Mrs. Lilac's Year

Paul I. Freet

iUniverse, Inc.
New York   Bloomington

Mrs. Lilac's Year

Copyright © 2009 Paul I. Freet

This is a work of fiction. All of the characters, names, incidents, organizations, and dialogue in this novel are either the products of the author's imagination or are used fictitiously.

iUniverse books may be ordered through booksellers or by contacting:

iUniverse
1663 Liberty Drive
Bloomington, IN 47403
www.iuniverse.com
1-800-Authors (1-800-288-4677)

ISBN: 978-1-4401-3448-7 (pbk)
ISBN: 978-1-4401-3450-0 (cloth)
ISBN: 978-1-4401-3449-4 (ebk)

Printed in the United States of America

iUniverse rev. date: 4/15/2009

For my Sister, Betty Morrison,
The real Betty Lilac,
With Love and Appreciation

JULY

Our journey begins in the heart of summer. The tunnel through which we pass is too narrow for turning back, but the real adventure lies ahead of us, always ahead. July is warm and lazy, and who could ask for more than that? The fast, high-stepping months are ahead, the ones that never tire and carry us with them in their confounded hurry. When they come, I will deal with their boundless energy, but for now I will keep July, cherish its still shimmering warmth, bask in the pungent summery air.

From Mrs. Lilac's Journal

Betty Lilac sat at the old farm table in the center of her living room, a cup of steaming coffee at hand. It was just after 9AM on a bright Monday morning as she sat sizing up her first client of the day. It was a woman of about 50, of medium build, dark curly hair, wearing shorts and a blue simple blouse. On the phone, she had given her name as Mrs. June Simmons. Mrs. Lilac hadn't asked where she was from. Her face wore a too easy smile and a rather expectant look.

Mrs. Lilac's spirits sank. Although dressed the part, in a purple dress and a thin silk shawl, with a colorful purple lace ribbon in her hair, she was not into reading the Tarot this morning. She had had a restful weekend, and getting back into the groove was not going to be easy, especially with a stranger who was obviously expecting a lot from her.

"I've heard so much about you, Mrs. Lilac," the lady gushed. I could hardly wait to meet you."

"Are you having a specific problem," asked Mrs. Lilac. "Before we lay out the cards, is there any particular issue you might want to take a look at?"

"Oh nothing in particular, I just want you to tell me everything you see, especially any good things that lie ahead!"

Mrs. Lilac's spirits sank even further, and she hoped her mood didn't show on her face. It was an oval shaped face, ringed by wavy medium length hair, a mixture of dark brown and gray. There was a touch of sadness around the eyes. Mostly, she was a happy sort, with a sense of humor and a ready smile, but this morning the smile was gone, but for the hint of it around the full lips. Somewhere in her late fifties, Mrs Lilac's age was always hard to read.

She was a bit heavy set, shorter than she liked at five feet four. She made up for this by wearing heels when she could, at least when her tired feet allowed. But she was pretty in her way, and most people thought her attractive and easy to be with.

It was always easier if the client came with a problem. She was very good at helping with relationships, for instance. Any question posed to her was easier than looking at the cards without a clue, and then finding the right path of a story that would satisfy the client. No, thought Mrs. Lilac, it was not going to be an easy morning.

Mrs. Lilac took the deck of cards into her hands. Almost automatically, she began shuffling them. Her eyes glanced off to the left as she shuffled. The morning sun streamed in the window. From not far away, she heard the muffled roar of machinery from the construction company up the road. The air coming in the front door was cool on her bare legs. She wished she could be outside with Scrappy her dog and Stormy her cat, sitting by the stream in the muted light, just plain old Betty Barnes from Altoona Pennsylvania, instead of sitting there on that uncomfortable chair, half-heartedly playing the part of Betty Lilac, card reader, extra-ordinaire. The name Mrs. Lilac had been given to her by her clients years ago when they found the cottage full of bouquets of lilacs from the bushes outside. It seemed an appropriate title for her, and it stuck.

Mrs. Lilac handed the cards to her client with a sigh. "Shuffle them for me, "she instructed. "Then separate them into three piles in front of you."

Mrs. Simmons separated the cards with a slightly shaking hand. Mrs. Lilac reached for them with a sinking feeling.

She always felt like that when she first took the cards into her hands. There, at the edge of the unknown, she was never sure of what she would see when she laid them out. Anything? Nothing? But as soon as she laid out the first card, she began to "see". The deck she used was The Rider Waite pack. She had many decks of cards in a dresser drawer in her bedroom, but she went back to this particular deck again and again. It was colorful and user friendly. The images brought no fear or dread to the clients mind. It was the first deck she had ever used.

She had come across it one day in a dusty old bookshop in Caronsburg. She had had a bleak time in her life, cancer of the breast, and after the misery of the diagnoses and treatment, and the subsequent anxiety that had held her captive in the house for what seemed like months, one day she woke up and realized she was bored with illness. She dressed and went out into a new day, and ended up at the bookstore where the cards nearly fell into her hands. That had been fifteen years before, and now a slow stream of clients always managed to show up at her door when she needed the few dollars they would "donate" for her service. There was an ancient law on the books in her state that said one could not charge for reading anything, card, moon, star or hand. But Mrs. Lilac managed to get by.

Mrs. Lilac had always been a mystic. She had prophetic dreams and had been interested in the stars since she was a girl. She had a kind of awareness when a particular person was about to call, or when she thought of a person they would surely turn up at her door. But she was in her forties before the cards came into her hands and revealed their mystery and magic to her.

This morning the cards were quite lively. A single layer of the Celtic cross told her quite a bit about her client.

"You have had quite a lot of lessons in your life," Mrs. Lilac began. "And you are not as happy at the moment as you would like others to believe. I see you at a kind of crossroads. You obviously are married, but it looks as though your children are grown and have left the nest. It looks like you possibly could have two, a boy and a girl. Your life seems like it is a little empty right at the moment. And your husband seems preoccupied. Does he drink?"

Mrs. Lilac stopped and let her eyes move from the cards to her client's face. The woman's appearance had changed. It now held a sad, sober look, and there were tears glistening at the corners of her eyes.

Mrs. Simmons nodded without a word, and Mrs. Lilac went on. Already, her earlier dread of the reading had lifted, and her indifference of the client had changed to a compassionate nature, which seemed to be the driving force of whatever wisdom or help she had inside her to give. It seemed to be the thing that brought total strangers to her and past clients back to her again and again.

"But don't despair, dear, the future looks quite bright. I see at sometime you will find a job, perhaps something part time, that will keep you occupied. And at this stage, you need to be busy.

As for your husband, his drinking seems already to be effecting his health. If he doesn't quit, he will surely suffer much in the end."

" Now, my dear," Mrs. Lilac changed directions, "always remember, I see only the future that you show me by shuffling the cards. Up from the depths of the subconscious may come something of what has been, what is happening now or possibly can be in the future. But you have the ability to change the way your future will go. Your life on this plane is like a vehicle, and you are its

3

driver. But, like any journey, some things may come to us without warning, and it is how we handle these unexpected events that build character, create wisdom. This is why we are here, to grow and to change into better spiritual beings. Astrology, the Tarot, are the maps that we can use along our way."

The lady stared across the table at her as Mrs. Lilac paused and took a long sip of her coffee.

Mrs. Lilac sensed that she was amazed and sobered.

She went on interpreting the cards. Mrs. Simmons asked a few questions, gave her some information. She talked about her husband, how he still worked in construction but began drinking the moment he arrived home in the evening and continued until long after she had gone to bed.

"It's a terrible habit," Mrs. Lilac, said, after a moment of silence when Mrs. Simmons had finished. "Your husband is also very mean when he drinks, and his abuse of you is obvious. Has he ever hit you?"

Mrs. Simmons shook her head. "No, but he's threatened, and he says terrible things and calls me horrible names."

"Why do you stay?" asked Mrs. Lilac.

"There's no place I can go. And I have no job or income. I spent my life taking care of the kids and taking care of him."

" It's a sad thing," said Mrs. Lilac. "I had it in my family. And you don't seem to have anyone to talk to about how you feel. You did once. You had a very sympathetic woman in your life. Was it your mother?"

Mrs. Simmons began to cry. Tears streamed down her cheeks, and Mrs. Lilac offered her a tissue from the box she kept on the side of the table. Oftentimes, her clients cried during the readings. Sometimes Mrs. Lilac cried quite a bit herself. This morning, however, there was deep sympathy, but no real tears. Alcoholism angered her, and when it appeared, she usually greeted it with a few choice, well placed words.

"How long has she been gone, dear?" Mrs. Lilac asked in a soft voice.

"About five years. I think of her every day. She was my best friend."

Mrs. Lilac stared at the cards. It looked as though someone else may have died in the past. A younger person. Perhaps in a car accident. The cards were jumbled, a page, the Chariot reversed, the Tower. Something happened at night. There was darkness, danger and fear. Mrs. Lilac turned again to Mrs. Simmons.

"Was there another loss in your life, a daughter, sister, friend?" She asked. Mrs. Simmons wore a blank stare. Mrs. Lilac told her what she had seen.

Still Mrs. Simmons shook her head.

"Perhaps it's something that will come to you. Maybe someone your husband knew. In any case, I want you to know things will improve for you

4

before the end of the year. Think about going out to find that job we saw. And perhaps counseling could help. Turn to yourself for a moment. Work at strengthening you. Your husband is beyond your help. He has a nasty habit that will kill him if he doesn't seek some help of his own."

And that was the end. The client was gone. Mrs. Lilac sat for a long moment at the table reflecting on what was seen and said. She always over-analyzed her performance. Could she have said something kinder? Could she have phrased something differently? Could she have misinterpreted what she had seen? Of course, she knew she was never completely right about what the cards showed her. She was human, and though she did think at times of her readings as a performance, she tried so hard in the end to give each person she saw, an uplifting thought, a bit of hope.

There were no more clients until later, but this one had taken quite a bit out of her.

Mrs. Lilac came back to herself. The morning light still streamed in the window. There were birds singing, and from somewhere far off a dog barked. Behind her, on the sofa, Scrappy, the West Highland White Terrier, stirred and looked at her with half-opened eyes. His tail wagged, and in an instant he was on the floor at her feet. He knew there was no client to come just now, and he seemed to want a walk. From the bedroom came Stormy, the Siamese. His blue eyes sparkled like diamonds, and he spoke to her in his high-pitched voice. "Can we go outside now?"

Sometimes, Mrs. Lilac thought Stormy believed he was a dog, and since he was the oldest, at eight, he felt he was the boss of the house. And although Scrappy was the larger of the two, he allowed the Siamese his Alpha position. He was just happy to be alive and have a warm and safe home. And over the years the two of them had become fast friends.

Mrs. Lilac stood up. She removed her shawl and her shoes, and led the pets out the front door and onto the small porch. Just beyond, in the driveway, sat the old battered blue Volkswagen Rabbit she had driven for years. Scrappy and Stormy ran ahead, past the lawn chair and the pots of red geraniums that flanked the front door. Mrs. Lilac followed them around the cottage and down across the sloping lawn toward the stream that flowed there quietly through the trees. It was called Rainbow River, after the trout that inhabited its cool depths, but it was really only a creek and not more than a couple of feet deep in any one spot.

The lawn was overgrown as usual. Even though David Garner, her young friend from one of the farms further along her road, tried to mow it for her weekly, the grass was almost uncontrollable so near the stream. But what did it matter? The grass felt wonderful under her tired feet, and the smells from the moving water, and the meadow beyond, were exquisite at this early hour. Chores, and especially grass mowing, could wait.

The cottage sat along a country road a couple of miles from the town. Across the road, there were fields and marshes, stretching away to the hills beyond. In the other direction, about a half mile away, were the first of several farms that stretched away into the distance. The cottage sat in a small grove of trees, and below it, and across the stream, was a huge meadow, actually a cow pasture for one of the farms. Mrs. Lilac's nearest neighbor, about a quarter of a mile away and in the direction of the town, was Gately's Construction Co. Mr. Gately was her landlord.

Mrs. Lilac had lived in the cottage now for nearly twenty years. Had it really been that long, she wondered, settling into an ancient lawn chair, having reached the edge of the stream? The dog and cat were already frolicking there in the muted sunlight that filtered in through the trees above. She had found the place right after coming to Caronsburg. An ad in the newspaper had led her to it, and the first time she had seen the gray shingled cottage sitting there in an overgrown thicket, it had spoken to her. In fact, she had seen the place in a dream when she still lived in Altoona, in the hell of a former life. She had actually visited it from above where she seemed to be hovering near the ceiling of the living room as her things, her furniture and a stove were carried in. On the actual moving day, she remembered the dream.

During her early years in Altoona, where she had lived in an apartment on the third floor, she had always dreamed of such a place. A place where she could be one with the natural world. As she was now, just sitting there letting her eyes drift over the meadow where cows grazed in the distance, and nearer at hand where Scrappy began to bark at a small flock of mallard ducks that was drifting downstream. At the first bark, they lifted one by one into the air above them.

Mrs. Lilac loved the stream bank. It was her escape from the reality of the world, its hurts and pain, and in the past few years, a place of renewal after even an hour or two of listening to the problems that crossed her table every day. And here on this cool July morning, it was a piece of paradise. There was an old picnic table under the trees, some wooden lawn chairs, and a swing hanging down from a tree above. Mrs. Lilac used to sit in it before she gained a little weight, but these days only an occasional child swung there while its parent had their cards read inside.

Here in the filtered sunlight, Mrs. Lilac felt she was the queen of her world, and indeed she was, in her bare feet and fly-away hair, here among the jewelweed clumps and the singing birds and chattering squirrels above her in the trees.

At the edge of the stream, Mrs. Lilac saw the weeds move, but Scrappy and Stormy were now lying silently at her feet. Probably Shing Shing, she thought. And she waited while there were a few more movements of the greenery and then all was still again. Shing Shing was a cat who had once lived with Mrs. Lilac, or the other way round for that matter. She was eighteen years old when she died in the corner of the bedroom, and Mrs. Lilac had been wracked by grief for weeks, until she discovered that even in death Shing had not left her. One night, Mrs. Lilac awoke to scratching at the window, and the next day she saw a flash of gray at the edge of her vision. Shing was still with her, and even now, on this exquisite July morning, she was still here at the edge of the stream, as she had always been when Mrs. Lilac ventured there. The other animals seemed to accept the fact that she was there from time to time, for she obviously spent the days wandering along the stream and across the fields and thickets as she always had. It gave Mrs. Lilac a sense of comfort knowing she was still there.

Across the stream, the meadow stretched away for what seemed like miles. The cows that lived there kept it cropped quite nicely. Just beyond the fence, a tree had been cut into chunks by the farmer. A storm had felled it, and although it was sad to lose a tree, Mrs. Lilac was glad the wood would be put to use. Several times, during the years Mrs. Lilac had lived there, a storm or a long period of heavy rain had sent the stream flooding out across the meadow. Since the cottage sat on slightly higher ground, the flood had never touched it, although a nasty hurricane had once brought it within reach of the back door. Mrs. Lilac had found refuge at a motel in the town until it had subsided, but usually the stream was peaceful and flowing quietly, as it was this morning. A short distance further along, it fell into mild rapids and curved in the distance. It was several yards wide and a couple of feet deep at the spot where she stood.

The cottage and this enchanted place were her whole world. At the edge of the cottage yard, and in the direction of the town, was a huge junk and storage yard, also Mr. Gately's property. The animals loved walking there, and so did Mrs. Lilac, for it was a lovely place to wander in. A narrow dirt track ran through it, and in the summer some of the older machinery hulks were covered with vines, honeysuckle and wild roses. She was always afraid that somewhere amidst all that loveliness there were also rats and snakes and a hundred and one dangers that could possibly harm her pets. So, usually in the late afternoon, before any clients showed up, Mrs. Lilac would put on Scrappy's leash, and they would go there for a brief hour of wandering.

Scrappy looked up at her now and seemed to whine longingly, his ears straight up, and Mrs. Lilac knew instinctively what he was thinking.

"Not now, dear," she said. "We will walk later. Let's just sit here quietly for awhile."

Mrs. Lilac was suddenly tired and her head nodded for a moment. The sound and smells of summer were wonderful to behold, and it all seemed to put her into a kind of meditative state.

"Betty, Betty Lilac!" It was a female voice, high pitched and insistent. Scrappy barked loudly and then ran to great the unexpected guest.

Mrs. Lilac sat up in her chair, suddenly quite awake. She hadn't heard the sound of an approaching car. It was her friend, Fern Gilmore. Fern was a widow who Mrs. Lilac had met years ago when she worked in town. They had been friends ever since. How many times had she told her to always call before coming out to visit? She looked toward the cottage and saw Fern come around the corner in all her glory, wearing a yellow sun dress and a huge wide brimmed blue hat, carrying her paintbox and easel over one arm and a large baggy purse on the other. She hurried her pace when she saw Mrs. Lilac. Fern was a tall woman, with gray hair pulled into a tight bun. A huge smile usually controlled her face, but this morning the smile was gone, and she looked quite worried.

"Don't get up, Dear, I'll come to you," she called, tottering down the slope.

Mrs. Lilac's spirits sank. She liked Fern; her oil paintings were magnificent. One of them, a huge study of daisies, hung above Mrs. Lilac's sofa. They had been friends for many years, but Fern was quite batty at times, and as absentminded as any living woman she knew. She always showed up unannounced and was impossible to get in touch with, either her phone was never answered, was disconnected, or the answering machine was full. This morning was just not the time for entertaining Fern.

"Whatever is wrong, my dear," asked Mrs. Lilac, trying not to let her feelings show, as Fern came up to her chair, huffing and puffing and wiping her brow with the back of her hand. She sat her burden of bag and box and paraphernalia down on the picnic table, and sank herself dejectedly into one of the chairs. She sat there for a moment catching her breath, and Mrs. Lilac wondered what new problem had befallen her. Fern always had some sort of muddle in her life and often called on Mrs. Lilac to consult the cards on her latest disaster.

It's Grayson," she spoke at last, tears streaming down her cheeks. "She's disappeared."

Grayson was Fern's cat, quite an aged tabby, and Mrs. Lilac knew she spent quite a lot of her time these days under the bed in the bedroom of the house in town where she lived with her mistress.

"I got up yesterday and went about my business as usual. I remember opening the door for a moment while I poured myself a cup of coffee, and it was then that I realized my baby wasn't there. Oh, Betty. You must look into the cards and see where she has gone. I searched the house through. Last night I stood on the porch and called and called, but there was nothing. You know I live so close to the road. I'm afraid she's been killed!"

"Now Dear, don't get overexcited." Mrs. Lilac soothed. "We'll go back to the house, have some coffee and a slice of pound cake. Then I'll see what I can in the cards."

A few moments later, they were sitting comfortably in the living room. Fern sat with a large slice of cake and a begging Stormy at her feet. Huge cups of coffee sat steaming before them both. Each of the animals took a thin sliver of cake from Fern's slim hand, before Mrs. Lilac was able to pick up the cards and lay them out in a seven card spread, a shorter version of the Celtic cross. She had no time or energy to read extensively for Fern today, and she knew at once on viewing the cards that the cat was not dead. The Sun and the World were in prominent positions. She also knew that housebound cats often had a desire to go out and live for a short time in the natural world they had viewed with longing from the window.

"She'll be back, dear," Mrs. Lilac said, after taking a long sip of the steaming brew. "Probably within three days. She's obviously having a lovely time, lying under a bush somewhere. You mustn't be so upset about this. Remember the last time she disappeared? You found her in the basement in the middle of a mousing expedition."

Fern began to calm down at once. Her eyes brightened and she sipped coffee and ate the last of the cake. "I think I'll do a bit of sketching by the stream," she said at last. "I brought my things, and I thought I might begin a small oil, if you don't mind."

Mrs. Lilac was thrilled by the thought of Fern's going down by the stream for awhile by herself. Fern's visits were always like this, she realized. She came and went as she pleased, and it was inevitable that she always brought a problem with her. But then, there were always those times when she came out of her mental fog, stepped up to the plate and was a real friend, as she had been at the time of Mrs. Lilac's illness. Fern had been there on a daily basis, doing bits of housework, bringing food and offering endless bits of encouragement. When given the challenge, Fern never failed her, and Mrs. Lilac had no reason for wanting her out of her life completely.

Much later, Mrs. Lilac, along with the Scrappy, Stormy duo, lay across her bed and fell asleep. When she awoke it was after three, and Fern was gone. Looking out the window toward the creek, there was no sign of her, and there was no evidence of any of the paraphernalia she had brought with her.

Mrs. Lilac had three or four clients scheduled for the evening, so she decided she should get up and get some chores done. By this time the afternoon warmth had settled in and Mrs. Lilac turned on the air conditioner in the living room window. Just then, Scrappy came flying to the screen door with a loud series of barks, and Mrs. Lilac hurried to see who had arrived.

It was Mr. Gately. He had driven up in an old pickup truck with the Gately Logo, and he was slowly walking up the driveway toward the front door.

Mr. Gately was a tall, medium sized man of about fifty five, with a bald head and a serious face. A cigar hung from his lip. He was wearing a green outfit with a large grease stain on the chest. He had never been a very friendly man, and a word or two was all she had ever managed to get out of him.

Mrs Lilac was silent as he approached. It was not often that he came to see her at the cottage. And she always paid the rent at the Construction Co. office. Whatever could he want to tell her?

"Mrs. Barnes," he said, stopping at the edge of the porch to speak to her. "Or is it Mrs. Lilac today?"

Mrs. Lilac said nothing, but a strange feeling seemed to creep over her as she stood there.

She felt a sudden chill in spite of the warm day.

"I've come here to let you know I have been thinking seriously of making some changes here on the property."

"Changes?" Said Mrs. Lilac, her voice steady. "And how would that effect me?"

Mr. Gately threw his cigar to the gravel drive and stamped in with his booted foot. "What I mean is, I'm thinking of expanding the equipment yard. I need more space. We are seriously thinking of tearing the cottage down. You have a lease for several months yet, so I'm here to let you know I would like you to be moved out by the end of May, next year."

It seemed to Mrs. Lilac that the world suddenly stopped. Her voice was gone, her arms wouldn't move, her feet felt as though they were lead. She reached out to steady herself by holding unto the roof of the old blue Rabbit.

Mr. Gately seemed not to notice how shocked his words had left her. "Besides," he went on. "There is a lot of talk around town these days about you. I've known for a long time about your cards and the readings you do. They say in town that you are dabbling in black magic. This is a small community, Mrs. Barnes. People talk. I'm trying to run a business here. I can't afford to have your bad reputation ruin what I have here."

After what seemed an eternity, Mrs. Lilac spoke. "I've lived here for almost twenty years, she mumbled. "Bad reputation? Black magic? That is totally insane. I am a respectable woman. I have a moral character that is decent, refined..."

"All the same," Mr. Gately went on. "I have made up my mind. If necessary I will have my lawyer send an official letter. But I think you are a smart woman, and I believe we can handle this between the two of us. My mind is made up. You have plenty of time to make whatever arrangements are necessary."

Mr Gately nodded, turned quickly, and was soon backing out the drive and heading back the way he had come.

Mrs. Lilac was like a statue, but somehow she managed to sink into the chair on the front porch. She was in shock for a moment, everything still around her, and then, bit by bit, the world came alive again. The color returned to the geraniums, the little maple tree began waving its leaves in the breeze. Birds called, the sound of machinery reached her ears from the construction yard. At her feet Scrappy lay silent, staring up at her. The look in his eyes told her he knew something was wrong.

"It will be alright," she said quietly. "Everything will be fine. Yes, fine indeed."

Mrs Lilac didn't know how she got through the afternoon and evening. She didn't remember if she ate anything. She had planned making pasta, but it was nearly dusk when she found herself at the table in the living room, the last client gone, the cards in a disheveled pile in front of her.

An empty coffee cup sat by her hand. The room was growing dark and the sounds outside were muted, insect noise and a car engine revving in the distance.

Tired as she was, Mrs. Lilac felt almost compelled to lay out a spread of cards for herself and her situation. She found it very difficult reading for herself. In the early days, it had somehow been easier, but as the years passed, she found reading for herself like looking through a glass darkly, a flash of truth here or there, but never a really true picture of what was to come. Perhaps it was her own emotions at that moment that might cloud things. Like now, she thought, laying down the first cards. And her first glimpse of them was dark, fear, anxiety. The Tower had a prominent place, and death. But somehow there was a bit of a story in the cards representing the future.

After great stress, joy, after a hard trail of tears, a final destination that was a happy place.

Perhaps it meant that in some future place she would find happiness again. She would stick to that promise, and perhaps at a more calm space in the next few weeks, she could look at the cards again. One worry she had with what she saw just now, was something like an illness, a hospital and great worry. While she was in fairly good health herself, and very seldom visited a doctor, she could see how the stress she was facing now could lead to a personal physical crisis.

But she focused on the final thought that there would be happiness again in her life. At times, that bit of hope was all she had to offer her clients. At this moment, it was all she had to offer herself.

Scrappy pawed at her leg. There was no sign of Stormy. Mrs. Lilac finally stood up and moved around the room turning on the lamps. She still felt numb, but the mind was coming alive again. In the kitchen, she poured some iced tea and took a long sip. Nothing in the house had changed. The kitchen was fairly clean, very few dishes needed to be done. She had planned some cooking and laundry, but nothing had been finished. The cake she had shared with Fern still sat on the table. On the wall, her Grandma Moses prints were as bright as ever. It was in her mind that all seemed dark and the sadness was palpable.

It was dark by the time she took Scrappy's lease, attached it to his collar and headed toward the road. She didn't feel as though she could walk far, but Scrappy needed the walk, and at her feet, Stormy also wanted to come along. Stormy was very good about staying close when they walked. Unlike Fern's Tabby, Stormy had quite a love of the outdoors. He often went off on his own adventures, but always came back home.

They walked up the road a short distance, the scent of wild roses and honeysuckle drifting in from the junk yard. They would not go in there tonight. Even though a huge full moon rose off to the left above them, Mrs. Lilac always loved the sight of the moon in summer, especially in July. She considered it her moon, since she was a Cancer and a sensitive soul. She loved her home, in spite of the fact that the cottage was old and falling down around her. It was still home, and now she knew this would be her last year in this enchanted place.

She could hardly stand going far on this night. Much against the wishes of her pets, she soon turned and led them back to the cottage.

Back inside, Mrs Lilac roamed about the house. The four rooms were totally familiar, a refuge. There, in the cupboard in the living room, were her blue willow plates and her collection of seashells. In a past life, Mrs. Lilac favored herself a pirate. In the bedroom were her books in stacks and piles, and her desk where she wrote her journal and composed poems when she had a chance. Mrs Lilac had several planets in Gemini, and this made her almost a dilettante with many interests. Over the years, she had fancied becoming an artist like Fern,, or a writer, or a researcher. In the end, her writing, the tarot readings and occasional bouts of crochet made up the corners of her world.

When she was finally ready for bed, and had lay down on the cool sheets and the lights were out, the two pets found their places next to her and snuggled close. They both seemed to sense her sadness. She suddenly realized it was not herself that she was sad for. She knew she could learn to live in another place. The clients would find her and come for their readings. It was the pets she felt sorry for, for this was their home. Neither of them had known any other place. Scrappy knew every corner of his world, the yard, the junk yard, the creek bank. Stormy knew it all as well, including places he went on his own and never shared with them.

But what about Shing, the precious cat had shared so many years of her life? What of her?

What if Mrs. Lilac were not there when the scratching came to the window? Who else would understand that the window had to be opened, even if no visible animal jumped across the void onto the bed? And what if the cottage were gone, invisible as her ghost cat?

While trying to go to sleep, Mrs. Lilac said a silent prayer to the universe for guidance.

AUGUST

There is a definite, perceptible slowing of life in August. The land lies lazy and lovely in the late afternoon sun. Is it my imagination, or do I detect just the slightest touch of Autumn in the weeds of the creek bank?
From Mrs. Lilac's Journal

August had turned dark. Mrs. Lilac stood at the window looking out on a late Thursday afternoon. The sky dripped rain and left round splatters etched on the window glass. Mist and fog lay along the meadow at places. It seemed as though there was no living thing left on the landscape. The month had started out to be sunny and bright, but even in that light, Mrs. Lilac had felt as though a darkness had descended, so that when it came, she was ready for it. It seemed her natural element.

Mr. Gately's visit had played over in her mind at least a thousand times during the past few days. But she had tried to keep busy. She had cooked and baked an assortment of cakes, cookies, rich stews, and had eaten too much as a result. And mainly, she had tried to concentrate on the clients who came to her for the usual advice. Today her first reading would be at four o'clock. A young lady by the name of Nancy, with a voice so low she could hardly hear her on the phone, was coming for a consultation. Mrs. Lilac felt it had something to do with the girl's health, for she remembered something that had been said about a doctor's appointment the following week.

Just then, the phone rang, and Mrs. Lilac turned from the window of the small sitting room where she had been standing. She sank into the large wicker chair that sat near the phone extension. Mrs. Lilac had three phones in her house, since she sometimes took a little longer than usual to pick one up, and people would often hang up after only three or four rings.

"Hello," said Mrs. Lilac, The line was silent with the exception of a radio or stereo playing in the background. And there was just the slightest hint of breathing. "Hello," she said again, but again no one answered. The music in the background continued to play. It was some orchestral piece she could not recognize.

Mrs. Lilac finally hung up the phone. She looked down at the fabric of the brown dress she was wearing and picked at a piece of lint.

Perhaps that is the girl who is coming at four, she thought. But then, she wondered if it might have been Fern trying to reach her. She had not heard from her friend since the day she had come with the problem of the missing cat. Perhaps she should try to get in touch with her in case there was something wrong.

Mrs. Lilac dialed Fern's number, which she knew by heart. She expected to hear the usual garbled message on the answering machine, but instead, and much to her surprise, Fern picked up the phone on the second ring with a cheery hello.

"Good afternoon, Fern," Mrs. Lilac began. "Did you just try to reach me?"

"No dear, I was just getting ready to go out for a bit of shopping. Is there something wrong?"

There was quite a bit wrong in her world, but Mrs. Lilac didn't want to share that with Fern at the moment. It might be more than she could handle just now.

"No, nothing, really. Someone just rang me, and when no one spoke, I thought perhaps it might have been you."

"You know I always make it quite clear that it's me when I call," Fern answered. "I'm a bit paranoid myself with strange phone calls."

That's obvious, thought Mrs. Lilac, remembering the terrible time she usually had when trying to get Fern on the telephone. Especially when there was a real need.

"By the way," said Mrs. Lilac, suddenly remembering the lost cat. "What's happened with Grayson?"

"She came back the very next day, of course," Fern answered. "She was waiting on the porch when I got up the next morning. I thought I told you."

Mrs. Lilac shook her head as she put the receiver back on the hook. It was just like Fern to worry her like that. But then the cards were fairly sure the cat would come home. It seemed Fern's muddles would never change.

She turned to go back to the living room, when the phone rang again. Mrs. Lilac hesitated before picking up the receiver. Already a bit of worry was creeping up her back. But she couldn't be afraid of the phone, and she picked it up again.

Once more, she could only hear that faint music. No voice answered, even when she spoke, "Hello, Hello," as loudly as before. Again, she hung up the phone.

She was still standing there in the middle of the room, when she heard a faint rumble of thunder roll across the meadow in the distance. The rain at the window sounded louder than it had all day. Scrappy was suddenly at her feet, and she reached down to pick him up. He had never liked storms, and she held him close and comforted him as he whined softly to himself. Mrs. Lilac suddenly felt a bit of panic at the back of her mind. Was it the coming storm or the phone calls that had spooked her?

Mrs. Lilac went back to the living room and sat out the storm on the couch with the animals. Stormy didn't mind the loud crashes and bangs, but Scrappy lay his head close to her with each one.

Finally, it was over, and Mrs. Lilac went about the house preparing for the evening to come. She tried to forget the strange phone calls while she freshened her appearance and put on a colorful blue dress for the readings. She placed a bright blue comb in her hair and slipped three or four gaudy rings on her fingers. Mrs. Lilac liked rings, and she had a great many, some expensive gold and silver, and others set with colorful stones. Some of them were just dime store acquisitions, but her clients remarked over and over again about how much they liked her rings. Today, she chose stones to match the color of her dress. Mrs. Lilac usually enjoyed dressing the part of the card reader. It seemed to always help when her clients viewed her as a mysterious presence. But to her it wouldn't have mattered if she appeared in jeans and a blouse for all her readings. She was just plain old Betty Barnes at heart. But the world was indeed a wide, mysterious place, and everyone needed a little fantasy. So if her appearance set the mood for the readings, it was all right with Mrs. Lilac.

At almost exactly four o'clock, Mrs. Lilac heard the sound of a car, and a knock came to the cottage door. The girl who stood on the porch was just a wisp of humanity, very thin, and about five feet two with wide eyes and a serious face ringed by short black hair. She was dressed in jeans with a blue sweater. Although the storm had passed, the rain still dripped from the roof and the maple tree, and the girl seemed anxious to be out of the falling drops.

" I'm Nancy, and you must be Mrs. Lilac. It's good to finally meet you," the girl whispered, when they were comfortably seated at the table. "Please forgive my voice. I'm slowly losing it, you know."

"What happened to it, dear," Mrs. Lilac inquired, sympathetically.

"I had some sort of virus that has paralyzed my vocal cords. The doctor says I will eventually lose it completely."

Mrs. Lilac had to strain to hear the girls words even though they were sitting so close to one another.

"That's why I've come to see you," the girl said. "I want you to tell me if there is any hope at all that I might recover."

Mrs. Lilac took up the cards and after the both of them had shuffled, she began laying them down on the worn oak table. They were bright, cheerful; the Sun, the Wheel of Fortune, the Star. Images began appearing in Mrs. Lilac's mind.

"This is not hopeless," Mrs. Lilac said as she began to read the story the colorful cards were telling her. "You must tell your Doctor there is someone else, a specialist that he must send you to. This is a person who lives somewhere a distance from here. But I think there is a cure for the problem you have. Don't give up. Let your doctor know you believe there is help out there for you."

The girl's face softened with Mrs. Lilac's words. She seemed relieved. After that, there were several other questions and a half hour or so passed before the girl hugged and thanked her and left.

During the rest of the evening, through four other readings with totally diverse people, Mrs. Lilac's mind kept going back to that young girl. She was sad about her fate and hoped that what she saw in the cards was true.

Mrs. Lilac did not believe in trying to fool any of her clients in any way. So many readers she had heard about used fakery in what they tried to do for others. The old stories of spells and dark clouds bored her to tears. And the requests by some readers for large amounts of money to do work for their clients, was nothing more than criminal as far as she was concerned. The charges for burning candles was ridiculous. She knew this was why it was against the law to charge for readings in her state.

Mrs. Lilac only described the stories and visions the cards helped her to see. She knew she was not always right. She had learned long ago that each individual was responsible for their own fate, the driver of the vehicle they used on the journey of life. The cards showed Mrs. Lilac what each of her clients were thinking of, in what direction they were going at the time of the reading. And oftentimes, they showed clear pictures of the future, good or bad. She always told each person that there was a possibility that she could be wrong, or might misinterpret what she was shown.

And there were always clients who seemed to touch her in some way, and it was hard to get these off her mind. Before she left, Mrs. Lilac had asked the young lady if it was she who had tried reaching her on the phone that afternoon. The girl had given her a blank stare and shook her head. So, before falling asleep that night, Mrs. Lilac spent quite a long time rerunning the sound of the young girl's whispering voice, along with the strange music she'd heard that day on the telephone.

The next morning all signs of the rain and the dark sky were gone. The sun shone brightly outside the kitchen window, the birds sang, and the air was clear and cool. Mrs. Lilac was led by a kind of radar to the creek bank, the two pets circling her like mad things. The grass was still wet, but what did it matter? The smells of the damp earth and the slightly high stream were like a balm for her frayed nerves.

The creek bank had become, for Mrs. Lilac, a kind of sacred place. It was here that she was close to nature and close to God. Since Mr. Gately's announcement a few weeks before, Mrs. Lilac had come here quite often to pray. She had asked the universe for guidance. If she was to stay here in her beloved cottage, she had asked for help to find a way. And, if she was to go, she had asked to be shown the proper direction.

When she had first moved in, the creek bank was nothing but a jumble of brush and weeds. It had taken her a few years to get it cleared so that she could have her sacred place. One bush at a time, one clump of brush and driftwood, and finally, with the help of David Tarner, her young neighbor, the day came when there was nothing but a velvet carpet leading to the water. Mrs. Lilac imagined a water goddess inhabiting the stream. She often believed that Gods and Goddesses were born in the mind. Oftentimes she would speak to the stream as though it heard her. It was a part of God, after all. And if she wanted to imagine a goddess living there, what did it matter? Each person had a small spark of God, living within. At least that was what Mrs. Lilac thought. Sometimes she would throw a few sticks into the water as a kind of offering. Or a smooth stone, or a slice of bread that she knew the ducks would get. Mrs. Lilac very seldom attended church, but the creek bank, there under the huge maple trees, was her cathedral, and, this morning, the cup of coffee she carried with her was like holy water. Mrs. Lilac believed she could be close to God where there was anything natural, beautiful. To her, the creek bank was holy ground.

She stood there by the edge of the water for a long moment, praying silently to whatever ears might hear. Off across the meadow, a long line of cows grazed silently. Far off in the distance, she saw the huge red barn and farmhouse of her nearest neighbor. And, in the other direction, she could see a thin line of dark rooftops where the town began, a couple of miles away.

Her cup of coffee had cooled by this time, so she threw the last of it into the stream as an offering to the water goddess, before going back to the house.

Sometime later, Mrs. Lilac was stirring up a chicken salad for lunch, when a knock came to the door. Hurrying there, she was surprised to find an acquaintance from town, Annabelle Wilkins, huffing and puffing on her porch.

Annabelle was a tall, black woman of about 60, from Mississippi. She was in town nursing her sister who was suffering from pancreatic cancer. Her prognosis had been that she might live for a year, but Annabelle had kept her alive for two. She insisted she would cure her in the end. Annabelle was a kind of herbalist, she made potions from an assorted array of greens, weeds and flowers. It was obvious that she was out right now searching for more of nature's offerings, for she was carrying a huge wicker basket for foraging. She was dressed in a large, loosely fitting, red and yellow flowered dress, a huge straw hat with a colorful scarf wrapped around the brim, and a pair of sturdy brown sandals. She also carried a huge wicker purse with a large rabbit foot hanging from the handle. A huge pair of dark sunglasses hung from a string around her neck, and her hair was done in thin dread locks all the way around, each one decorated at the end by shells of varying sizes.

"Ms. Lilac," could you please let this tired stranger in?" Annabelle asked, "I'm fallin' over out here. I walked all the way from town, and I'm just about done in."

Mrs Lilac graciously helped the large lady inside. Breathing heavily, Annabelle sank into the center of the sofa and started to fan herself with a magazine she found lying on the coffee table. Mrs. Lilac hurried to the kitchen and poured the visitor a colorful mug of steaming coffee. She also brought along a plate of sugar cookies she had baked a couple of days before.

It wasn't long after she'd had a few sips of good coffee and a brief rest, that Annabelle was her usual self again. She looked at Mrs. Lilac in that odd, almost sideways glance she had. It was a look that seemed to pierce your very soul. Her one eye was also larger than the other.

"Mrs. Lilac," said Annabelle, "what kind of a name is that? Where did you get that awful name? Seems to me they shoulda' called you Mrs. Nightshade, Mrs. Slippery Elm, or some other such name like that." She laughed, with a high pitched laugh. "Down south where I come from, we girls didn't fool around with any of that sweet stuff. We did what we did, and we meant business. If someone crossed us, we knew what to do about it. I always say there's only one thing wrong with you. You're just too nice. Be like me, honey. People think I'm nice, but underneath, I'm as swift and

19

mean as a snake and wicked as a spider." She laughed again, her whole body shaking, as she held on to her coffee cup for dear life.

"Honey, I'm out here today for more of my materials, you know what I mean. Everything seems to be used up, and I'm gonna go wander down along the stream there and find me some real fine ingredients. People just seem to need Annabelle's medicines more than ever right now, and my sister is doin' just fine, thank you. That old cancer is a shrinkin' and I got it on the run."

She looked at Mrs. Lilac again with that strange hard look. She turned her head from side to side as though she were looking at her up and down at the same time. Mrs. Lilac always found it interesting and fun to be in Annabelle's company. She had visited with her many times since she had come to town. The original visit had been to have cards read about her sister's health. Mrs. Lilac had greeted her cards with caution and guarded optimism. Today, however, Mrs. Lilac's mood had not risen in spite of her friend's good natured fun, and Annabelle seemed to notice. She usually enjoyed giving her a good laugh.

"What's goin' on with you, honey," Annabelle asked, her voice suddenly deep and serious. I know there's something wrong with you, girl. Now tell Annabelle all about it."

"No, there's nothing wrong. It just may be the weather," Mrs Lilac answered.

"The weather, my rabbit's foot. There's something dark and deep brewin' in you. I can see it, I can feel it. Old Annabelle knows things, Old Annabelle can see things, too. Now what is it girl?"

Mrs. Lilac suddenly burst into tears. They ran out of her eyes in a flood. Annabelle was instantly on her feet, a wad of tissues in her hand.

Now, now," she said, "Just let the dark come out, honey, just let it go. Tell old Annabelle all about it."

When the tears subsided, Mrs. Lilac told her about Mr. Gately's visit and about her having to give up her home.

Annabelle sat silently on the sofa with a dark look on her face. Several moments passed before she spoke. "And what do the cards say, honey? What do you see there when you lay them down?"

"You know it's very hard to read for myself." Mrs. Lilac dabbed at her eyes. "The sight goes out the other side somehow. They do seem to show I'll find a happy place somewhere."

"This just won't do," Annabelle said, shaking her head. "This just ain't right. Down where I came from there's a little thing called voodoo. I don't often mention that in this crazy place, they're so high and mighty up here, that they might just try to escort me right out of town." She laughed again, although it was a serious kind of a laugh and her body remained taut. "I had a husband one time, deed I did. He was a real sneaky type, womanizer, drinker, you know what I mean. Well, he made a mistake one day, he took his fist to me, left some bruises on my face. I did a little work then, with the help of an old woman I knew. She lived in the swamps down there, and we did a little magic, a twist of this, a turn of that. Within three months that mean snake was lying dead on the street with a heart attack."

Mrs Lilac said nothing. She liked Annabelle; she had a good heart beyond her sassiness. She also knew from some of their past talks that her friend delved into some things that Mrs. Lilac didn't believe in. In her mind, anything could happen if a person believed in something deeply enough. She knew it would do no good, however, to disagree or challenge Annabelle's beliefs or practices, especially today.

"I'm gonna take care of this for you," Annabelle said, standing up suddenly. "I'm going down here to the stream now and I'm going to fill up my basket. I'm going to pick me a little bit of this and a little bit of that. I'll find enough for my potions, and a little extra for my poisons, and some night at midnight, I'm going to walk back out here and do a little work for you. Now don't you worry none, honey. You won't know when I do this, it's my thing, all mine. I enjoy putting things to right. I see the evil eye. I know how to use it a little."

Annabelle left then, carrying her basket down toward the stream. Mrs. Lilac sat there for a moment, then got up and went about preparing lunch. She was a bit disturbed at herself for getting so emotional in front of her guest. She realized it was the first time she had really allowed herself to cry over Mr. Gately's decision.

A lunch of chicken salad sandwiches and strawberry cheesecake, was laid out on the pine kitchen table when Annabelle returned, sometime later. Her basket, which she left on the porch, was piled high with greenery and roots. Several dark black spiny things stuck out from one side.

Mrs. Lilac served them a tall glass of iced tea with lunch, and Annabelle ate and drank heartily. Her laughter filled the kitchen. By the time she left, an hour later, Mrs. Lilac's spirits had risen quite a bit. She hadn't really wanted a guest, but she was glad Annabelle had dropped in. Upon walking out the door, Annabelle had whispered a few words in her ear. "Evil is evil and good is good. You need to stay in the middle of the road, honey. Let old Annabelle go into the ditch." She was still laughing as she went out the driveway and started up the road toward town.

Before her evening readings, Mrs. Lilac lay down on the bed and took a nap. The visit with Annabelle had tired her, and she fell asleep quite easily.

Perhaps it was Annabelle's talk about voodoo and her dead husband, but Mrs. Lilac dreamed she was in the dark. None of the lights in the house would come on, and a knock came to the door. At the same time, the phone rang. She was making her way slowly through the dark house toward the front door when she woke up. Her heart was pounding, and it took her a few moments to come to herself. It was quiet and still but for Scrappy's tail slapping the bed from where he lay beside her. Stormy sat comfortably on the window sill where the late afternoon sun was still streaming in.

In spite of the dream, she came back to herself and felt fairly calm again. Even the few readings of the evening went well. It was just before nine when she was finished, and the pets were eagerly waiting by the door when she finally stood up from the table.

It was a fine evening for a walk. The day had been cool and breezy and, as the darkness slowly made its way over the landscape, the moon rose, nearly full. Mrs. Lilac took deep gulps of the delicious summer air as Scrappy pulled her toward the road.

It was a narrow road that led toward town, but it was paved. In the other direction, it wound past several farms and rejoined a larger road a few miles beyond. Not many cars passed by, especially at night. It was usually just the local farmers. During the day, trucks from Gately's Construction Co. and an occasional tractor and wagon passed. So, that in the evening, she could walk with the pets with little fear that a car might come along and run them over. The road toward town was fairly empty of houses until one got closer. An old cemetery lay some distance beyond Mr. Gately's lot, on the opposite side of the road. Not that she was afraid, but Mrs. Lilac used it as a turning place for their walks. She was usually winded by then anyway.

The animals loved the walks along the road. An occasional rabbit would set Scrappy to pulling on the leash. And Stormy would go running into the thick underbrush from time to time. Mrs. Lilac found the walk, especially tonight, refreshing, the coolness of air and the summery scents of the season relaxed her, healing her frayed nerves.

They reached the entrance to the junk yard, but Mrs. Lilac decided it was not good to go there tonight, though Scrappy pulled her in that direction. It made a lovely walk during the day, especially when there was no one working at the construction company. After dark, there were too many creepy crawlies about, and Mrs. Lilac had no desire to find herself in a compromising position.

Darkness had fallen by this time, though the moon rose high above them and lighted the way, and she felt it was best just now to stick to familiar pathways. They were nearly up to the old graveyard when she saw the lights of a car heading in their direction. Mrs. Lilac pulled Scrappy to the edge of the road, but Stormy had temporarily disappeared on one of his own adventures. Meeting a car along the road was not an unusual occurrence, but this one seemed to be going awfully slow, and, when the headlights caught her, it slowed down even more. Mrs. Lilac reached down and picked up a very squirmy Scrappy, who chose that moment to begin barking. The bright headlights blinded her momentarily, and the car stopped in front of her. She could hardly make out the model, perhaps a Cadillac, a dark brown or black. She could make out the dark form of the driver, but the window seemed to be tinted And just when she expected the window to open and a lost driver ask for directions, the car suddenly moved forward and finally crept by her. Mrs. Lilac followed the car as far as she could with her eyes before the road curved behind them.

Then she turned and finally was able to spot Stormy creeping out of a clump of underbrush nearby. Something told her it was time to turn back toward home anyway, since they were over a half mile from the cottage. Just as she did, she saw the headlights through the trees. The car had turned and was coming back in their direction. Mrs. Lilac, acting instinctively, headed toward the graveyard, which was just a short distance away. She walked as quickly as possible, nearly running, carrying Scrappy, with a skittering Stormy at her feet.

The graveyard didn't scare her; she realized it was the living that one was to be afraid of, but going in the open gateway, with moonlight streaming down on the pale white stones, spooked her a little. The car was getting closer. She heard the engine and the lights were growing brighter. Mrs. Lilac saw a particularly large stone just off the gravel pathway, and quickly hunkered down behind it. Scrappy was silent now, as though he knew to be still and quiet. She only hoped Stormy would not be seen, wherever he was.

The car crept by the cemetery. Mrs. Lilac didn't actually see it, but heard it very clearly from where she was hiding. It seemed to her it may have actually stopped at one point, but she couldn't be sure. Her mind picked up a hundred odd sounds, limbs creaking, bushes moving. In a tired mind, it sounded like a hundred lost spirits moaning at once.

Why is my heart racing so hard, she wondered. Was it the car or this strange place that brought the most fear? Finally, it seemed to her all was quiet. She cautiously stood and saw that the car was gone, the roadway lay empty in the moonlight.

Without another thought, Mrs. Lilac made it out of the cemetery and headed toward home at a fast pace. No more cars or obstacles of any kind lay ahead of her. Several minutes later, breathing hard, she reached her own driveway. She stood there quietly, until her breath came easier and more normally, before going inside. She sat Scrappy down, and had taken off his leash, before realizing that Stormy was also there safely beside her. She made sure the front and back doors were both doubly locked before she sat down to collect her thoughts. It would be a long time before she fell asleep that night, she realized.

She went to bed and tried sleeping anyway. She was very tired, but somehow her mind didn't cooperate. So, as she always did at such a moment, she got up and heated some milk, then went about the house looking over her collections, the favorite books, the blue willow plates, her flowered English tea cups, displayed for all to see in the old yellow chest in the living room. And in the kitchen were her Grandma Moses prints that meant the world to her. Such a peaceful world the artist had created. If only hers was that peaceful just now.

She sat down at her table in the usual place. The warm glow of the lamps attempted to calm her. Mrs. Lilac shuffled her cards. What did she want to know? Who had made the strange calls earlier? Was there anything to be feared from the strange car on the road? Oftentimes, in the past, she wondered if she was safe living out here. An occasional friend or client had mentioned their concern. Her position was a strange one, she realized. There was danger in what people thought of her. Sometimes people tried to harm the thing they feared.

Mrs. Lilac lay out the cards. They were dark, as usual. A puzzle. Someone was afraid, terrified, in fact. Was it her? She continued to lay down the cards. No, someone might be afraid of her for some reason. After a struggle of some sort, there would be an eventual solution, wisdom.

Mrs. Lilac lay down the cards and shook her head. Finally, she took the glass, with half the milk left, and rinsed it in the sink. The window above it faced the fence of the Construction Co. yard. Suddenly, she saw a flash of light coming from that direction. But it was a flicker and nothing more. She stood for a moment peering into the darkness, but there were no additional flashes. There was no sound from outside but the gentle movement of the trees swaying in the breeze. Was the flash of light her imagination? Perhaps she had seen a falling star through the underbrush.

Mrs. Lilac said a quiet prayer for guidance and went to bed thinking of the peaceful haying scene in one of her Grandma Moses prints.

SEPTEMBER

September in the countryside is corn being cut in the fields and apple trees hanging heavy with red and yellow fruit. It is the rampant growth of wild flowers at the roadside, the Queen Anne's Lace and still more Black Eyed Susans, and tall yellow flowers I can't identify.

From Mrs. Lilac's Journal

September brought flocks of strange black birds to the creek bank and the meadow. Stormy went crazy at the window trying to get to them. On a late Saturday afternoon, after her readings were finished, Mrs. Lilac stood behind her cat staring out the sitting room window at the strange birds. They came and flew off in waves, their high pitched calls and chattering was disconcerting. It was a hazy afternoon, the sun was weakened by the overcast. Off across the meadow, she saw the first autumn coloring on a few trees.

A kind of depression had fallen over Mrs. Lilac in the past few weeks. A sort of acceptance had settled in her mind, but she had made no plans of any kind. A couple of times, she had looked at the newspaper ads for rentals, half-heartedly, but had laid the paper folds down, because looking at them left her with such a sad, hollow feeling.

The days had passed quietly and uneventfully. She had chided herself quite often for the fear she had felt over the strange phones calls and the dark car and driver that had caused her to hide in the cemetery that night. She had actually laughed over it a couple of times as she prowled the house picking up after herself, or did the dishes at the sink in the kitchen. It was a laughing matter in broad daylight, but her walks after dark were limited to a short distance, either side of the driveway.

Yet nothing out of the way had happened, no more strange phone calls, no more mysterious cars and no more lights in the junk yard. One day had followed another. The only thing that had changed was the number of clients who came. Three might come one day, four the next, and the problems were always the same, in one way or another, the most popular being the subject of love, which Mrs. Lilac was quite good at helping with. She seemed to have the understanding and compassion that brought folks back and back again. Will my boy friend return? Is the relationship over? Will I get a marriage proposal?

Of course, there was always the unusual problem, or the unusual person, that caused her to really use her mind and concentration in the way she lay out the cards.

One such individual arrived at her door that very afternoon. She was still at the window watching the dark birds when she heard a knock. Since she hadn't been expecting anyone and had no appointments, the sound of it was a kind of shock and a surprise to her.

It was a strange man, a sober, sad looking man, dressed in plain jeans and a long sleeved blue work shirt. He had light hair, thinning on top, looked about fifty five, to Mrs. Lilac's discerning eye, and was slightly overweight for his nearly six foot frame. But his face had a pleasant, vulnerable look. He was still handsome, but in his youth he must have been a striking figure.

He had been wearing a work cap and took it off as Mrs. Lilac opened the door.

"Are you Mrs. Barnes," he asked, with a shy kind of voice.

"Yes, I am, " she said. "Will you come in?"

He nodded, and Mrs. Lilac stepped aside, not sure of what to make of her visitor.

"David Tarner, told me about you," he went on, when Mrs. Lilac had sat him at the end of her table. She naturally sat down at the other end. "He said it was customary to make an appointment, but I was passing this afternoon, and I thought you might be at home. If you'd like, we can set up a time and I can come back."

"No, it's okay," she said, "we can talk now," sensing by the man's voice that there must be something that was concerning, probably bothering him, and she didn't have the heart to turn him away. "Any friend of David's is okay with me. David is a great young man, he's helped me around the house quite a bit in the past few years. Do you live around here?"

" Yes, and by the way, my name is Bill Green. I live about five miles from here. My farm is actually in the next township. David and his father have helped me with the harvesting and planting from time to time. I have a diary farm, and I milk quite a few cows."

"I assume you'd like to ask me a question or perhaps you have a problem," Mrs. Lilac, began, "but I'm sure David has told you, I always like to consult the tarot first."

She handed him the cards and asked him to shuffle and to clear his mind. "Think only of that which you wish for, " she said, "don't concentrate on negative things that have already occurred."

Mrs. Lilac, in a flowered house dress and an apron, certainly wasn't dressed the part of the reader today. Even her hair was tied in a kind of white kerchief, because she had been cleaning earlier. But her mind was already working, and after Mr. Green handed her the stack of cards, and she started laying them down, she immediately began to get thoughts and images.

A terrible sadness came out of the very first cards she lay down. "You've had a great loss," Mrs. Lilac began, "a sorrow. You are still trying to deal with the pain. There is a woman here, the queen of cups, reversed. She's no longer in your life. I see illness around her, and I think she has passed."

She looked up at Mr. Green. He nodded his head and already his eyes were tearing up.

"Was she your wife?" Mrs. Lilac asked softly.

Mr. Green nodded his head. Already, tears were streaming down his cheeks. Mrs. Lilac quietly offered him a tissue from the box that was always handy at the side of the table.

"How long ago did you lose her?" asked Mrs. Lilac, when he had gained his composure.

"It's been almost a year," Mr.. Green said, his voice breaking from time to time as he spoke. "But my sorrow and pain seem to be getting worse instead of better. I think about it every moment of the day. She had cancer, and suffered very much near the end. I couldn't help her. That's the worst thing. I keep seeing her taking those last breaths. I was with her at the end. Our children were there, too. They're grown and gone and that makes it even worse. I do have a twelve year old grandson who comes and helps me now. It's good he's there, but I miss her so much."

Mrs. Lilac quietly continued to lay out the cards. She began to speak again after a few moments. "You must believe me when I tell you that your wife has gone to a beautiful world that we can't even begin to imagine. Her suffering is ended, and she is happy again. She is, of course, still concerned about you, and she wants you to try to find happiness again. Naturally, it would be silly of me to tell you that can happen just now. Your grief is a process that only time can bring you through. It may take you another year or more, but the day will come when you will stop remembering the sadness of her last days, and only think of the joy and happiness that you had together. That is the woman you will always hold in your heart, that is the love death cannot take from you."

She paused, noticing that tears were still falling from Mr. Green's swollen eyes,

"You have been through the worst of this already. Nothing you face in the future will be quite as terrible or as sad."

" Now I'm going to tell you something that you may not be ready to hear, and you may not like it that I say it. But I will say it anyway. The future cards in your layout look very good. I see great happiness for you in a year or two. And this is what the cards are telling me, another woman will come into your life at some future time. Oh yes, she will, don't shake your head no. Time is a great healer. "

Mrs. Lilac's voice had changed tone, the subconscious was in total control at this moment, and she could not stop herself even if she tried. "And don't even think that that would be betraying your wife. You were a wonderful husband to her, of course as we all do, you had faults, and that is what is bothering you so much. You never gave your wife some of the things she wanted from you. She told you often that she would like to travel, that she would like the two of you to do some fun things together, occasionally. But you were a kind of workaholic, most days, and never had the time to give her some of the simple things she asked for."

Mr. Green lowered his head and held his hand to his eyes.

"But your wife loved you completely, for all your faults. She still does, and she would like nothing more than your finding another to share your life with. She only wants you to think of her as happy and fulfilled where she is, in ways that none of us can be here."

"Now, once again, your current grief will eventually pass. Be patient with yourself and stop agonizing over things that no longer matter. And while it does show respect to go to the grave where you left her, your wife can hear you anywhere you chose to speak to her."

Mr. Green's body was now wracked with sobs. Mrs. Lilac stood up quickly and went around the table to pat him on the shoulder. "There, there, it's okay," she said. "It's good to cry, it's good to let our grief go, as much or as little as we can. You will find happiness again."

"Thank you," Mr. Green said, standing up quickly and dabbing at his eyes. "I"ll think about what you said."

"And be sure to come back again if you think I can help you."

He nodded and left hurriedly after laying some bills down on the table. Mrs. Lilac shook her head and watched him through the window as he backed the pickup he was driving out into the road.

She knew it must have been embarrassing for him, a grown man, to cry before a perfect stranger, but she was glad he had been able to share a little grief with her. She knew it would help him in the end.

After the gentleman had gone, a quick look at her watch told her it was nearly five o'clock. The way Scrappy was prancing around her feet let her know he thought it was time to go outdoors. Since it was daylight still, and there was no one working at the Construction Company just now, they could easily take a walk through the yard without danger of any kind.

So she quickly attached his leash, and they were on their way. She didn't know how Stormy knew it, but whenever they were ready to go outside, he was always there, wherever he might be hiding in the house, and was ready to come along. Since he had his own personal litter box in a corner of the bathroom, his desires for the outdoors were completely different than Scrappy's.

The lower entrance to the construction yard was only a short distance up the road from Mrs. Lilac's driveway. She enjoyed the brief walk along the road. The sun still shone weakly through the haze, but the air was surprisingly cool. A slight breeze was blowing as they walked. The roadside was lined with flowering plants and weeds. It had been a summer of rampant growth, and the Queen Anne's Lace was everywhere, interspersed with teasel, thistle and ragweed. But it was beautifully colorful, and Mrs. Lilac loved seeing and smelling the lush foliage that was all around them as they walked. An occasional rabbit went bounding into the thicket, causing Scrappy to bark and pull at his leash. Birds were everywhere, in constant motion, singing and calling, and insects buzzed around them. Sometimes the flies and mosquitos were pesky, but today she didn't seem to mind.

Stormy bounded ahead of them as they neared the open gateway that led to the yard. The upper yard was close to the construction buildings and the lower one cut through the land nearer to Mrs. Lilac's cottage. In fact, the end of it was only a few yards from her, but a chain link fence separated the two properties.

A narrow dirt road circled the lots, and this is what Mrs. Lilac followed on their forays there. And this time, as always, when they started along the track, she said "Oh, how lovely," in a quiet voice. The storage yard was a wonderful place for walking through. There were a thousand places for Stormy to explore, and hundreds of scents for Scrappy's pleasure. Mrs. Lilac found it slow going with Scrappy's desire to smell and mark everything in sight. The foliage, both along the track and at the edge of the yard nearest the stream, was spectacular. Vines covered some of the older, unused machinery, and cattails grew in a boggy area close to the water. The section of the yard closest to Mrs. Lilac's cottage was her favorite, because the hulks of rusty old machinery had been covered over the years by an interesting array of vines, and trees in every shape and size grew in the most unlikely places. At the spot where they came nearest to the cottage, Mrs. Lilac stopped to catch her breath. She looked toward the fence and noticed that the weeds had been trampled there, as if someone had gone into the underbrush. She walked closer and saw that it was only a short distance to the fence. Beyond was the cottage, quiet and still in the sunlight.

Had someone gone over to the fence to look across at the cottage? One of the workers perhaps? But for what reason? She stared down at the trampled pathway through the weeds. Nearer the dirt track, two cigarette butts had been tramped out. Someone had been there at some point. The light she had seen that night would have been coming from this spot.

Perplexed, Mrs. Lilac walked on. She told herself she must not let this silly thing she had found get to her. Mr. Gately had many workers who often came to the yards for many different reasons. Obviously, the person who had lingered there for a cigarette was one of his workers. But then, what could they possibly have hoped to see by going through the weeds to the fence to stare across the distance of a few yards to the cottage?

The birds were still rising and falling like smoke when she got back to the cottage, leaving her with an uneasy feeling. She must remember to ask her friend David about them when he came again to mow her grass, also about Mr. Green.

She thought about her visitor of that afternoon. David had told him about her, he said. Mrs. Lilac never really knew if David believed in what she did or not. He enjoyed talking to her about many things and often ate the food she offered when his work was done. But she had the feeling that perhaps his parents might not agree with what she did. The families in the area were often set in their ways. But now she knew David had actually sent someone to talk with her. It would be interesting to ask him about it when she saw him next time.

The opportunity came the following Monday afternoon. David was in his senior year at the high school in town, and stopped at her house on the way home from school. He usually rode the school bus, but on this day, he was driving his old, beat up pick up.

David gave her a big smile when she answered the door. Scrappy barked excitedly, because David was one of his favorites. After finishing the mowing, David usually put the leash on Scrappy and went running with him along the road for a distance. Mrs. Lilac always watched them with enthusiasm and wished it were still within her power to run like that. David was tall and lanky with close-cropped blond hair. Actually, it was a cross between red and blond, and he had a few freckles to go with it.

"Hey, Mrs. Barnes," he said. David never called her Mrs. Lilac, and she had often asked him to call her Betty. But his greeting was always the same. "Thought I'd get your lawn on the way home. Do you mind?"

"Of course not," she said. "And drop in when you're finished. I'll have something for you to eat."

It was always good to hear the sound of the mower. David was such an energetic, ambitious young man. When he wasn't mowing for half a dozen or more people in the summer, he was working on his father's farm. He planned to go to college when he was finished with high school, but he surprised her once when he told her he might like to become a teacher. Farming full time was not his cup of tea. She had told him that she knew whatever he did he would be a success.

Later, when the mowing was done and Scrappy had had his run along the road, David came into the house sweating. Mrs. Lilac sent him to the bathroom to wash up, and then offered him a coke, a cheeseburger and some chips.

David ate it heartedly, along with a slice of coconut cake she had baked that morning.

After he had pushed away his plate, Mrs. Lilac brought up the subject of the birds. She had seen them here other years but never in the numbers of the past few weeks.

"They are migrating now." David told her. "It's been a kind of dry summer, and I think that's why they are visiting our stream in such numbers. Sometimes it reminds you of that film, The Birds, doesn't it? They'll be gone in a couple of weeks."

"Your friend Mr. Green dropped by on Saturday," Mrs Lilac said, after a brief silence.

"Bill?" He asked. "Yeah, I told him to come talk to you."

"Why David, I didn't think you took much stock in what I do."

David lowered his eyes, shyly. He raised them again and said, "Well, at first I didn't think much of it, but as I got to know you, I felt more comfortable about it. You know what a lot of people think about cards and all that. They think it's witchcraft and black magic, weird stuff. But they don't know you like I do. And I know you are a good person. I told Bill that. He's been sad, real sad, since his wife died. We've really worried because he hasn't pulled out of it, and sometimes when you talk to him, he's only half there. I told him you've helped a lot of people."

"You are so kind to say nice things about me," Mrs. Lilac said quietly, when he was finished and had lowered his eyes to his plate. "I do try to help where I can.   I'm not always right, but I give it my best.   I hope I can help Mr. Green.   He seems like such a fine man."

"Yes he is, Mrs. Barnes.   He's a good person, just like you are."   And he looked at her strangely.

Her first client that evening was Goldie Meyers.   She was a heavy set woman of about 70, wearing a pants suit of a fashionable blue color, her gray hair worn in a freshly coifed, shorter style.   Goldie was someone Mrs. Lilac had read for on a couple of other occasions.   She lived in an old mill in town where she had a large Antique store on the first floor, with her apartment above it.   She had sold antique furniture there for many years, but now she was ready to retire and was having trouble selling the building.

"Do you think I'll ever sell the mill," Mrs. Lilac," she asked in a whiny, distressed voice.

Mrs. Lilac had always felt that Goldie always got her way.   Her husband had died some years earlier of an undisclosed illness, but from the things Goldie had told her about their lives together, Mrs. Lilac was certain she had always had everything just the way she wanted it.   She had been trying to sell the mill for over a year with no luck, and now Mrs. Lilac felt there was a certain blame Goldie wanted to put on her readings.

"You've told me every time I've come that the mill was going to sell." Goldie continued, in the same distressed voice.   "You even said once that perhaps I'd have an offer within three months.   Well, dear, you've been way off!   I don't know why I keep coming back!"

"Perhaps it's because you just need to talk to someone," Mrs. Lilac replied. "It always helps to take your frustrations out on someone, and I guess I'm it."

"I know I sound mean," Goldie said, her upper lip curling as though she was about to burst into tears.   "But I want to move out to my house in the country and get out of this crazy town.   I've had it.   I've even tried to throw in the business and remaining inventory.   But no one, I repeat, no one, has been interested!"

Mrs. Lilac could almost imagine Goldie stamping her foot like a petulant child who hasn't gotten its way.   But she said nothing as she took the cards from Goldie's hands where they had been shuffled over and over for the past few minutes.

"Now if these cards don't show us something, perhaps you'd better go out and buy a new deck."   Goldie chided, as Mrs. Lilac began laying out the cards.

The first few cards showed some sort of blockage.   "There is something keeping the sale from happening," Mrs Lilac began. "Maybe its just the time element. You know it's so hard to tell time in the cards. The place will eventually sell. Being so close to the stream there, has the mill ever flooded?"

"Oh, that's not it!" Goldie snapped. "One of the hurricanes was bad, and we did have some water on the first floor, but it was easily cleared." She paused a moment, rubbing her hands in thought. "You don't suppose it's because the place is haunted?"

"Haunted?" Mrs. Lilac's head rose sharply.

"Yes, there's always been an entity there. Footsteps in the dead of night, upstairs and down. I even saw a misty figure in the show room one morning when I came down. Maybe it's driving people away. Is that possible?"

"I think it's possible your mill may be haunted, but I'm sure the ghost doesn't care if you leave it or not." Wickedly, in her mind, Mrs. Lilac thought, "Perhaps the ghost would like it if you were gone!"

"Well, the noises I've heard in the back room have been loud lately." Goldie went on. "I am always so nervous when the realtor brings a new person to look at the place. What if they hear the banging, or what if the ghost himself just comes walking into the room?"

Mrs. Lilac lay a few more cards down on the table. I just think there are many different reasons why your mill isn't selling," she said, in a soft voice, being as careful as possible not to upset her difficult client. "There are many things about the mill that are in need of repair. You even told me once that the roof required work and those storage rooms at the back are a mess. As for the ghost, I agree the mill may be haunted, but the cards seem to indicate a living presence may be causing some of the problem. When I look at the cards I see someone is hiding or hiding something from you. Again, I think you will have someone interested in the property before the end of the year. I'd like to come look at the place, someday," Mrs. Lilac concluded. "Maybe there's something useful I could pick up if I came to visit and looked around."

"Why that's a great idea,"Goldie cried, showing more enthusiasm than Mrs. Lilac had ever observed in her. "In fact, what would you think of a party upstairs in my apartment? Maybe next month, for Halloween. I'd invite a few friends, and you could read their cards! We could even try a seance! It sounds like a lot of fun. What do you say?"

"I'd be willing to try that," Mrs. Lilac said. "No more then ten people, though, you know it's difficult for me if the group is too large. Halloween is great, too, it will create a mood, especially if the decorations are nicely done."

Mrs. Lilac was glad when the card reading was over and the client had gone. She hated the difficult ones. She wasn't even sure why she agreed to attend the party, but then, she always tried to satisfy, and in spite of Goldie's pettiness, she always left a nice tip. And besides, she needed a getaway. The days had grown sadder as fall approached. Perhaps getting out among people would be a kind of elixir for her growing depression.

It was nearly dark, and Mrs. Lilac was fixing a snack in the kitchen after her last client of the day, when Scrappy's ears stood tall and straight and he began to bark. There was someone at the door, and Scrappy was there before the knock sounded. It was Bill Green. He stood there sheepishly with a large basket of apples in his hand.

"Mrs. Barnes, I... I wanted to thank you for talking to me on Saturday. I feel some better.

I have a few apple trees on my farm, and I wanted you to have these."

Mrs. Lilac took the basket, so surprised she couldn't think of a thing to say.

"Why they're lovely," she said at last, her hands shaking a bit. "I'll make something with them, a pie perhaps."

"You were kind to talk to me," he said. "If I can ever help you in anyway, please let me know."

He left then, after standing there awkwardly for a moment. Mrs. Lilac felt flushed. He seemed such a nice man and she felt so sorry for him. And he was still quite a nice looking fellow. Surely there was someone out there who would help give him the happiness he deserved.

"Oh dear, oh dear," Mrs. Lilac said to herself, after putting the apples in the kitchen and returning to the living room to sink into the sofa.. "This won't do."

It had been a long time since any man had touched her like that, awaking her compassion, sympathy, pity. But for her, that was dangerous ground. She had long ago decided it was best to ride out the rest of her life alone. Yet, how could she ignore the human side of her that occasionally came to the surface? And she realized suddenly that Bill Green seemed to have touched buttons within her that made her realize she was still alive.

Sometime later, after preparing for bed, Mrs. Lilac sat at her desk in the bedroom writing in her journal. Her hair was in curlers and she was dressed in pajamas and a tattered old robe.

"Only a few days until September ends," she wrote. "Where will I be next year at this time."

The ringing phone interrupted her, and she lay down her pen. She picked up her appointment book with one hand and the receiver with the other.

There was silence at the other end, and that familiar music. It seemed to be coming from a distance, and Mrs. Lilac felt her heart race.

"Do you know who I am?"

It was a man's voice, one she had never heard before. The words were whispered, and obviously, the speaker was trying to disguise his identity. The question seemed seriously asked, so Mrs. Lilac, trying to be calm, answered as seriously.

"No, I haven't the slightest idea who you are. Should I?"

But there was silence and the line went dead. Mrs. Lilac sat holding the phone for a long while, listening to the beep- beep. It took a moment or two until the shock lifted, and she could think rationally again.

But it was anger she felt, she realized, more than any other emotion, and she would not let it disturb what had started out to be a peaceful evening in late September. The caller was obviously a mental case, no doubt someone who took satisfaction from trying to frighten others.

She took up her pen again. "One of my clients brought me a basket of apples today," she wrote, "and I feel something stir in me again. What is it? Plain ordinary humanness, or just the simple joy of being alive?"

OCTOBER

October arrives in the night, and when I go out this morning his presence is everywhere. He arrives on waves of nostalgia, puffs of wood smoke and the first faint scent of burning leaves. It seems he has spent the first few hours of his visit touching the world with splashes of color, if for no other reason than to convince me once and for all that he is the one great artist.

From Mrs. Lilac's Journal

Mrs. Lilac went down to the stream many times as October began its slow journey across the land. She would sit there under the trees as the leaves began to fall, and stare out across the meadow while Scrappy and Stormy skittered among the mounds and piles that had already fallen. A few days into the month, Mrs. Lilac couldn't remember a year where the leaves fell so voluminously, and at night, she could actually hear them pattering down on the roof. On a night when she couldn't sleep, she wrote a poem about the leaves.

The autumn leaves fall swiftly now like tears,
yet I still recall the gold of other years,
the yellows and the reds, the blazing days,
the sunsets with their dazzling fire-like rays.
And once so poignant in a year so bright,
the falling leaves disturbed my sleep at night,
nearly like rain, the way they pattered down,
upon the world, upon the sleeping town.
They still fall softly in my listening heart,
what can be dead that echoes in the dark?
In rustling whisper, in myriad tap and ping;
in different octaves do their voices sing.

Now in an Autumn where my heart is sad,
I recall that music and my soul is glad.

On a bright Monday afternoon before her first reading, Mrs. Lilac and the pets made a bee line for the bank of Rainbow River. The creek was certainly in keeping with its name today. She was wearing a light sweater, for it was a bit chilly, as she stood there watching the leaves ride the current like multi-colored boats. Off across the meadow, she saw the bright trees follow the far stream like a line of soldiers. As many leaves as had fallen and continued to fall, there were still quite a lot of them on the tree limbs. The scent of the Autumn air was exquisite. The sound of the leaves falling and the breeze, were like a kind of enchanted music when mixed together. But today, autumn was sad and tear- filled for many reasons. Holding her sweater close around her, Mrs. Lilac prayed to the universe and her Goddess, for hope, help and guidance. Perhaps sensing her sadness, Scrappy came up to her and stood on his hind legs looking up into her eyes. Her heart melted. How could she tell him this splendid October would be the last they would spend in this magical place? She reached down, picked him up and hugged him to her breast for a long moment. Stormy was off at the edge of the stream chasing a leaf as though it were a butterfly. He was too enraptured with his own world just now to notice the tears that were streaming down her cheeks.

Her sojourn by the stream that afternoon lasted only a short time. She had clients coming and had to spend a few moments in the bathroom washing her face and trying to give the appearance that she was at least partly herself. She freshened her outfit of dark slacks and a brown sweater, by wrapping a bright orange scarf around her neck. She put on a pair of earrings to match, and several large stone rings in Autumn colors. At least she would look the part, even if she didn't feel it.

Her clients arrived just around six o'clock. It was Mrs. Rose Wilder and her daughter Serena.

Mrs. Lilac had done readings for the both of them many times. Mrs. Wilder was a librarian at the County Library in town, and Serena was a student at the nearby Allansburg State University, where she was a senior. Mrs. Wilder was in her early fifties, and always gave the appearance of being exhausted. She was tall and thin with brown wavy hair, and always dressed in dark, professional outfits. She was a lovely woman, Mrs. Lilac always thought, but she rarely smiled. And this evening she came to the door alone, her face even more lined with worry than usual. Serena would wait in the car until it was her turn, she informed Mrs. Lilac.

"I'm so worried about Serena," Rose said, as soon as she was seated at the table.

But I thought, she was doing fine," Mrs Lilac said, remembering her long bout with anorexia, and about her hospitalization and slow recovery, and then, of course, about her meeting the Graham boy at the local Drama Guild in town, where the two of them had been a sensation playing Anne and Peter in The Diary of Anne Frank.

"Everything you predicted for her came true, Mrs. Lilac." Rose began. "And you know I have thanked you over and over again for helping us both understand why she had that awful eating disorder. And then, above all, you told her she was going to meet a boy when she tried out for the play at the Drama Guild. And she met Bernie, and they were so happy." Rose burst into tears.

"What's happened," Mrs. Lilac asked. "Are they having trouble?"

"Yes, they just broke up last week. That awful Standish girl, Shirl, came home from college over the weekend and they reconnected!"

"I'm so sorry," Mrs. Lilac said, remembering Bernie Graham's former girlfriend, blond Shirl, who had left him for Roger Brandt the football hero. "What happened to the star quarterback? I thought they were happily engaged."

"Oh Mrs. Lilac, it's such a long story. I'm just so afraid this will set her back years. She's been doing so well."

Mrs. Lilac sat up straight, and took the deck of cards into her hands. She could see it was going to be a long evening. Much as she liked Rose, it seemed so many of her readings turned serious because there was always a problem or a muddle. Of course, she was sympathetic. She knew Serena had been through a lot. Her anorexia had been a long ordeal. She was the third of three children. Her two older brothers were the center of the family, and Serena had always felt put aside. They were both into sports, and their father, a school principal, pushed and promoted them and spent very little time with his daughter. It had all tied together in an eating disorder, but thank goodness, the therapy and clinic had brought the child through it.

"Let's not think too far ahead, Rose," Mrs. Lilac told her. " Let's shuffle the cards and see what they have to tell us about the situation."

Rose shuffled the cards hurriedly, and Mrs. Lilac began laying out the Celtic cross.

The first cards were hopeful. They gave her the instant feeling that the young couple would work out their problems and be reunited. She told Rose what she was seeing.

"Oh do you think so, Mrs. Lilac. I pray you are right."

"I think there was a problem there before Shirl came home from college," Mrs. Lilac said. "I think Bernie may have been a little clingy and controlling, and perhaps Serena, with her new found self esteem, may have been flaunting her independence a bit. It seems to me, Bernie may be turning toward his old girlfriend to get Serena's attention back where he wants it."

Rose's face relaxed a bit, and Mrs. Lilac continued to answer her usual questions, about her stressful job, which she loved, and about her husband and sons. Mrs. Lilac always tried being kind and sympathetic, but sometimes it was on the tip of her tongue to tell Rose that she had too much on her plate, that she needed to give up many of the hundred and one activities she was involved with and volunteered for. She knew in her heart that that had also played a part in her daughter's illness, and if she didn't stop burning the candle at both ends, it would someday effect her own health as well.

Rose was finally done with her cards, and she had a smile on her face and gave Mrs. Lilac a big hug as she left to exchange places with Serena in the car.

Serena came into the house smiling broadly. Mrs. Lilac was stunned. She half expected to see the thin waif of two years before, with wide sunken eyes and cheeks. Instead, Serena was practically glowing.

"Serena," Mrs. Lilac said, "You look lovely. By the way your mother sounded, I expected you to be a mess."

"Oh, Mother exaggerates, " Serena said. "I'm fine. I'm just angry at Bernie, that's all. He just doesn't listen to me sometimes. And he was trying to control my every movement. You know how men can be."

Serena sat down at the table, her dark eyes flashing. She pushed her wavy black hair aside, and Mrs. Lilac noticed the girl looked as though she had gained a few more pounds. The dark blue sweater she was wearing helped give her the look of health and vitality, a look that had been missing for a long time.

"That's why Bernie and I broke up. It really had nothing to do with Shirl coming home. I've changed, Mrs. Lilac, the therapy and counseling did wonders for me. I don't care what happens between us now, I'm just not satisfied by the way he tries to run my life."

"Oh, you still love him," Mrs Lilac said. "I know you do. Are you sure this can't be worked out?"

"I guess time will tell," Serena said, her voice suddenly more serious than it had been when she first came in. And Mrs. Lilac could tell, by the sad look that suddenly crossed the young girl's face, that the whole thing had effected her more than she was willing to admit at the moment.

" Let's do a spread of cards on the question," Mrs. Lilac said, handing the deck to Serena for shuffling. Serena took them and hurriedly mixed them two or three times before Mrs. Lilac began laying them down on the dark table.

"I see that Bernie is very sad about what has happened." Mrs. Lilac said, the cards making a slapping sound as she lay them down, one by one. "I also see him coming to your door very soon. He seems to want to talk this over. He says he has no feelings at all for Shirl, he is simply trying to make you jealous. He actually has thought of marrying you, Serena. Has he mentioned this to you?"

"Oh, he has talked about it. Together we've discussed it in a half serious way. We've even toyed with the idea of how many children we might like to have. But at this point, he would have to make some major changes before we would ever go too far in that direction. I have my career to think of. You know I have always dreamed of going to Washington to work in the political field in some capacity, and Bernie wants to go there, too. But he doesn't seem to have a direction right now, and he dropped out of college after two years. He needs to be more centered, have a career path for himself. I don't want him always living in my shadow."

Mrs. Lilac admired the young girl for her honesty and courage. She had overcome so much, and would overcome quite a lot more in the years to come.

" Talk to him, dear," Mrs. Lilac told her. "Tell him what you've just told me. The cards show the two of you will be reunited. As for marriage, I see that, too. Don't let stubbornness and unwillingness to change, cloud the bright future I have always seen for you both."

When the reading was finished, Serena hugged her hard and kissed her cheek. "You are such a dear, Mrs. Lilac. Thank You."

A hush settled over the house when the readings were finished that evening. Mrs. Lilac sat quietly in the lamp light for a few moments, letting her thoughts settle. So many things, both good and bad, surfaced as she sat there. She suddenly remembered the apples that Mr. Green had brought her, a couple of weeks or more ago. She had placed them in the refrigerator and had hoped to bake a pie or two with them. With a sense of urgency, she went to the kitchen and found that the bright fruit was still crisp and firm. She decided at that moment, that this was as good a time as any to bake a pie. She soon sat at the table sending long strips of apple peel into the garbage can.

She was humming by the time the pies were in the oven. The smell soon wafting throughout the house was heavenly. There were enough apples for two pies, and she suddenly thought of Mr. Green standing there on the porch with the apples that day. She knew what she was going to do with the extra pie. She would take it to him the very next day. She wasn't quite sure where the farm was located, but she could call David, or try to locate it herself. She decided on the latter, because she didn't want David to know that she was having such school girl thoughts about his friend.

The pies turned out beautifully. The crust was a rich brown, and she had decorated the top with some cut out apples she had made from the extra dough. She covered the pies finally with a cloth, and took the animals out for a last run before bed. It was a blazing autumn night. The stars shone as brightly as she could remember. The chill of winter's eventual return was in the air already, and the scent was sharp with the rich, pungent smell of earth and time.

She was nearly exhausted by the time they were all nestled snugly in bed. There was still the faint sound of leaves falling outside, but over all, the night was very still. She thought of her delivery of the pie the next day. It sent her heart racing just a bit too fast. She was somewhere between sleep and waking when the sound of scratching came to the window. She got up and half expected to actually find Shing sitting there on the sill. "Oh, it's sad, she thought, the things we must say goodbye to in this life, all the hurtful and painful things there are to remember."

She raised the window, and said very quietly, "Thank you, Shing, for not leaving me completely."

Yes, she thought, as she snuggled back under the covers where the two very real pets were already snoozing, we do lose many things in our lives, but there is always something new to dream of, and maybe, just maybe, some new person to come, who might offer something rare in the way of friendship and joy.

The next morning, the sun was streaming in the window quite brightly when Mrs. Lilac came awake. She felt rested as she dressed in a pair of blue slacks and a colorful tan and gold sweater. She paid special attention to her hair and make up, finally shaking her head when she realized that there was not much she could do in that area. The usual trip to the creek bank was quite invigorating this morning; the air was still chilly, the leaves fell in the breeze, and the scents were indescribable. The two pets acted like wild things and Mrs. Lilac felt as though she were a whirligig.

She was sitting at the table having a very welcome cup of coffee when the phone rang. It seemed in the past month, she was startled every time she heard the phone ring, but there had been no more strange calls since the night the mysterious man's whispering voice had spoken to her.

This time it was Fern. "Good morning, dear," she began, "and how are you this beautiful morning?"

It had been weeks since she had heard from her friend, and because of the way things had gone, Mrs. Lilac had seen no reason to go through the usual or unusual red tape to talk to her. So she had just been still, and as she knew she would, Fern had contacted her. Fern was a Gemini, and she seemed to have the habit of ignoring you for months and then would call and act as though she had seen you the day before. But that was Fern, and Mrs. Lilac understood.

Before she had a chance to say a word, Fern was off on her own. "I ran into that awful Annabelle character yesterday on the street. And she told me about your having to move. Why didn't you tell me? I felt terrible hearing it from a stranger. Why haven't you called me? I could be helping you here. I know a lot of people and could be asking around for you about a new place. When do you have to be out? And what will you do with the pets? Oh, this is awful. I can't believe after all these years, Gately would stoop so low."

Mrs. Lilac sat there, half listening to her friend, until she found an opening for getting in a few words. "I'm fine, Fern; I am getting along. I haven't gotten in touch with you because I've been so busy, and I didn't want you to worry You know if I needed you, I would have been in touch by now. I don't have to be out of here until Spring, so there is plenty of time for the two of us to get our heads together."

"Oh, isn't the weather lovely," Fern went on, without skipping a beat. "I need to come out there for a bit of sketching before all the leaves are gone. I'm out of ideas just at the moment, and I thought I might come out and begin an Autumn landscape, a small one, as I don't think I have the energy to do any of those large things again. How about this afternoon? Perhaps that would work for you?"

"Oh, not today Fern. I've too many clients, " Mrs. Lilac said. "But I have a Halloween party next week. It's above Meyer's Antique shop, and I'm going to read cards for about ten guests. Perhaps you could come out in the afternoon for your sketching, and then attend the party with me that evening. I'm sure Goldie won't mind if I bring someone. And you could help with the set up. I think we'll need some special outfits and decor for this one. What do you say?"

"Sound's like a nice idea." Fern agreed.

"It's Thursday evening," Mrs. Lilac said, "are you available then?"

"Yes, that's open," she answered, after a brief pause. I'll see you around two that afternoon."

The phone was silent and Mrs. Lilac stood up, shaking her head. It was always like Fern to pop into her life at a very busy moment. And just now, she had to get ready for the delivery of her pie.

It was just after eleven when she set out on her adventure. She knew Scrappy would have enjoyed the drive, but this morning, Mrs. Lilac decided it would be best to leave her pet at home.

The old Rabbit groaned as she turned the key, but it started, and Mrs. Lilac was careful to be sure the pie, which she had placed in a small cardboard box, was riding safely on the seat next to her. The drive down the country road was quite a beautiful one. There were still a few corn shocks here and there. Modern farming methods had taken away so much of the old ways, but there were dried corn stalks and pumpkins on porches, scarecrows and assorted bought decor in farmhouse windows as she passed. And everywhere, there were the incredible trees in their finest autumn dress, miles of colored woods stretching away.

She crossed the township line, and began checking out the farms as she passed. Some were simple and run down, a barn, a shed, another would be more complex with two or three large silos, and there were cows everywhere. The fields were littered with them in some places.

She was beginning to despair that she might not be able to find the place, when a sign at the end of a lane told her in large black letters that this was Green's Dairy Farm. She slowed quickly and turned in.

There was no one about as she drove past a long low barn and pulled in front of a two story brick house where several cats sat on the front porch. Her hands were trembling as she picked up the pie and got out of the car. She went up the walk, and was about to step unto the porch, when a voice from behind her said, "Good morning."

She turned and saw that it was Bill Green. He seemed surprised to see her, but at least, his face seemed a bit more cheerful this morning. He was carrying a bucket and was dressed in blue work clothing.

At first she was afraid that she might not know what to say, but she held out the pie to him and when he had taken it, with a long look inside the box, she was able to speak freely.

"I made pies of your apples and thought you might like one for yourself, so here I am. I had no trouble finding your farm, and what a lovely drive it was, coming here."

"This is quite a surprise," Mr. Green said." I've thought of you and your encouraging words often." And then there was a silence, and she realized he didn't know what to say. "Well, I hope you enjoy it, and now, I must be getting back. I have a busy afternoon."

Thank you," he said finally. I.. I appreciate your kindness. I"ll keep in touch."

"You do that," she said, finally, and went back to the car, feeling the flush on her face. He was still standing there on the porch, looking in her direction, as she pulled out of the driveway.

The day of the Halloween party, the sky was overcast. That afternoon, Mrs. Lilac stood at the window looking down toward the stream. The trees didn't look quite so colorful just now, and the wind was really setting the leaves flying. She wasn't quite sure Fern would show up, since sketching by the creek bank didn't look so promising, and as absent minded as she was, it was quite possible she had forgotten.

But show up she did. She arrived precisely at two. She was dressed in black slacks and a sweater to match, and carried only a small black bag and a very high pointed witch's hat.

"Too cold and nasty for sketching today," she said cheerily, "so I left all my art stuff sitting at home. I thought you and I could just have a cozy afternoon together, catching up! I thought I'd go to the party as a witch. Do you like my hat?" She put it on and paraded around the room, setting off a barking melee in an excited Scrappy.

Mrs. Lilac laughed loudly. It was the first good laugh she had had in days. Fern could do that to her. Dear Fern, batty as a bedbug, but always there when she needed her.

They had quite a fun afternoon. Fern was in rare form, and she helped Mrs. Lilac pick out her most intriguing fortune telling outfit. It was entirely purple, from a silk turban with a large amethyst in the center, to a colorful dress and jacket outfit to match. As for props, they choose a large crystal ball with a base of encircled gold angels, and a bright piece of purple felt to be placed on the card table.

It was already dark when Fern drove them into town at just after six o'clock. Goldie's place was ablaze with light. Candles shone from the windows, and a magnificent arrangement of corn shocks, scarecrows and pumpkins filled the front entrance. A side door led up to Goldie's apartment, and the rail was encircled by strings of miniature orange lights.

Goldie met them at the top of the stairs, wearing orange slacks and a jacket to match. "I'm a pumpkin," she said, hugging Mrs. Lilac and whispering in her ear. "I've got to talk to you. You won't believe what's happened. As soon as I get you settled, we'll talk."

Several guests had already arrived. They were gathered in the large living room which was decorated in festive colors. A few ladies were in costume, a pirate, a skeleton. Others were in plain, everyday dress. One lady was dressed entirely in pink feathers. She came up to Mrs. Lilac at once. "I'm the feather lady," she said, handing Mrs. Lilac a pink feather. "Have you had your feather today?"

Mrs. Lilac was speechless. She was glad that Goldie introduced her just then, and led her to a small room off to the side, with Fern following. "I'm putting you in here for your readings, dear. It's private and I think you'll be comfortable."

It was a nice, out of the way room for readings, Mrs. Lilac noticed. A small sofa sat along one wall, and a coffee table of lit candles in assorted colors, shapes and sizes sat before it. Plants of many varieties were placed here and there, and a card table and two comfortable chairs sat near a shuttered window.

'This will do very nicely," Mrs. Lilac said. "I've brought my friend Fern along for moral support."

"Oh that's fine. I've met Fern many times here in town. Let's have her get your things together while we go into my bedroom for a little talk."

Goldie's bedroom, at the back of the apartment, was a picture in pink and gold. Goldie closed the door and led Mrs. Lilac to a chair in the small sitting area at one end of the king sized bed.

"I think I've sold the mill!" she cried, when they were seated. "A man came in on his own two weeks ago, and I showed him around. He wants to open a motorcycle shop and dealership, and he thinks the whole set up is ideal for him."

"Why that's the best thing possible," Mrs. Lilac said, feeling buoyed by Goldie's good news.

"Yes, the papers are being drawn up now, and he's even put a deposit on it. He wants to be in by March 1st."

"Will that give you enough time?" Mrs Lilac asked.

"I think so. He seems very cooperative and I don't see a problem. But there's something else. You told me when you read for me that there was something hidden or standing in the way.

Well I found out what that was. It was my son."

Goldie looked down at her lap and rubbed her hands in a kind of sad, futile gesture. "My realtor told me, in confidence, that my son was here when she showed a couple of folks through. He works for me, you know. Delivers and picks up furniture. That kind of thing. Well, he was pointing out all the negatives about the place. A person would come in very interested, but by the time they left, they had changed their mind. It was Dennis, my son. And when I confronted him, it seemed it was true. He didn't want me to sell. I guess he thought I would turn the business and the building over to him in the end. But when I had asked him earlier if he wanted to take over, financially and all, you understand, he always said, definitely no. What he really wanted was a free ride."

Mrs. Lilac shook her head. There's nothing surprising about life, is there, dear? Well, good for you."

"And the strangest thing of all is this, Mrs. Lilac," Goldie said excitedly, " I kept hearing those strange noises in the back storeroom, so I had one of the policeman here in town go back there and investigate. And my goodness, he discovered a homeless man living clear at the back of the place. There was a kind of hidden entrance around there by the stream, and the old man was coming there at night and getting into the building. And you know, you mentioned in your reading about something, perhaps a person, being hidden. You are amazing!"

Mrs. Lilac could only think of the hard time Goldie had given her, the last evening they had been together. But she sighed with relief as Goldie hugged and thanked her. And as they went back to join the group in the living room, Mrs. Lilac felt a kind of weight lifted from her shoulders.

Armed with a cup of hot tea, Mrs. Lilac began her readings. She lost track of time and the faces became a blur. One lady in street clothes had a tragic story. Her husband had been killed in a railroad accident and was having trouble getting past it. The feather lady surprised her. Her name was Joanne Barkely. She was actually a very serious woman, a nurse who worked in the local hospital. The feathered outfit was actually a costume she used to go around to schools in the area to speak on proper hygiene and diet for young people. She had three children of her own, and a husband who was a workaholic. The only real problem she had was with a very sick mother who was unwilling to go into a nursing home. Mrs. Lilac told her to be patient, and eventually, the whole thing would come together and work out.

When the readings were finished, Mrs. Lilac joined the group in the living room and sampled some of the goodies Goldie had laid out on a table covered by a bright print cloth of colored Autumn leaves. She particular enjoyed a pumpkin roll, which was delicious, also a lovely vegetable platter of colorful pepper strips and other bits for dipping. Fern joined her. It seemed she had been having quite a good time, since she knew so many of the guests. Fern's artistic talents were well known in the community, and people often came seeking her out for paintings of themselves, homes or pets.

Sometime later, Goldie went to the center of the room and clapped her hands. "Anyone wishing to join myself and Mrs. Lilac, we are going to tour the downstairs to see if we can conjure up any spirits." She lifted a large Ouija board into the air. "And down in the main show room, we are going to have kind of a seance with the board to see if anyone wants to come through."

"Mrs. Lilac was glad they were going to tour the area where a ghost had often shown its presence, but she wasn't so sure of how she felt about the board. Some authorities advised against using them, due to the fact that they often attracted malevolent spirits; still, she was not afraid, since she had the motto that it was the living that one should be wary of.

Several of the guests chose to follow them to the downstairs store area. Goldie turned on only a few lights as they entered the main showroom. The different shapes of the furniture caused dark shadows to leap from every side as they walked. At the center of the room was a long dining room table set with about eight chairs. It was here that Goldie placed the Ouija board and pulled a large white candle to the center of the table and lit it.

"Mrs. Lilac," Goldie said in a low spooky voice, "you and Fern should be the ones to operate the pointer."

Mrs. Lilac protested, but the hostess wouldn't have it any other way, so she and Fern sat down at the table across from each other, and placed their hands on the board. They made quite a picture, Fern in her witch hat and Mrs. Lilac in her turban. Fern laughed, a high pitched laugh, as the pointer began to move, slowly at first, and then faster, as it began to go to various letters.

"Who is here with us," Goldie asked in a deep voice. "If you are here, tell us who you are."

Almost at once, the pointer stopped at the J. It continued on to O then H and N.

Mrs Lilac was watching the whole thing with deep curiosity. She stared at Fern from time to time. Was she moving the pointer? At least she knew it was going without her assistance. One or two of the ladies gasped when the pointer continued to move. It quickly spelled out the word S-t-r-a-n-d.

"John Strand," Goldie said. "What are you doing in my mill?"

Before they could continue, something landed on the table with a loud thump. Everyone screamed, including Mrs. Lilac. There was complete confusion for a moment. One of the women went running toward the exit. Mrs. Lilac held her hand to her breast, until she saw that the object was a very large, long haired, black cat.

"Jasmine," Goldie cried. "Oh my, you nearly gave us all heart attacks. I'm sorry folks, I should have warned you, my cat lives down here most of the time. I guess this is where she gets some of her choicest mice. She just wanted to see what was going on. Shall we continue?"

By this time, Mrs. Lilac, and Fern too, obviously, by the way her hands shook and her hat was askew, was ready to be away from this place. The readings had tired her, and now the Ouija board seemed more like a game than anything. But to keep Goldie satisfied, they went on with the game.

Soon the pointer was moving again. " I a-m s-i-c-k. It spelled out. W-a-n-t t-o g-o h-o-m-e.

"Where is your home?" Goldie asked.

I- n t-h-e s-o-u-t-h. I w-a-n-t t-o g-o h-o-m-e.

"What are you doing here," Goldie repeated.

F-I-g-h-t-i-n-g t-h-e w-a-r w-i-t-h t-h-e m-e- n. I r-e-s-t i-n t-h-e b-a-c-k. N-o o-n-e k-n-o-w-s I h-i-d-e. I a-m s-i-c-k.

The pointer stopped and wouldn't go on. Goldie urged it to continue, but there was no further movement. "Someone told me once the mill was haunted by a civil war soldier," she told those gathered around the table. "I don't know how they came to that conclusion. But it seems to me John Strand has spoken. I am a believer."

"Is there anyone else here who wants to come through," Goldie spoke again, quite loudly, her voice echoing about them. Mrs. Lilac held her breath.

Again the pointer moved and suddenly stopped at yes.

Then it moved to R-e-b-e-c-c-a.

"Rebecca who?" Goldie asked.

But again the board was silent for a moment. At last it moved again. I w-a-s k-i-l-l-e-d.

"How were you killed?"

H-i-t b-y a c-a-r.

"Oh my God," It was the Feather Lady. She stood up so quickly from the chair where she was sitting, that the whole table shook, and a feather from her outfit went dancing about the room. "That's Becky, my daughter Trina's friend! She was killed last year!"

Without another word, the Feather Lady sprung up from the table and rushed out of the place. The other participants also rose and scurried away. Mrs. Lilac had the feeling that she and Fern suddenly had the plague. Only Goldie laughed and acted as though nothing unusual had happened. She went out with the departing guests and returned to her apartment. Mrs. Lilac and Fern looked at each other and shook their heads. They were last to leave the cavernous storeroom, and the rest of the evening passed in a blur.

Fern drove off in a rush as soon as they made it back to the cottage, and Mrs. Lilac finally found herself alone. She was very tired and her feet ached, but the animals still needed to go out. Mrs. Lilac could barely follow Scrappy and Stormy to the creek bank. She took the flashlight with her, and the eerie light on the water, and on the scampering animals, was disconcerting. Specters seemed to dance around her in the dark, and fear and foreboding came at her from all directions.

She realized her nerves were a bit frayed. The readings and the Ouija board revelations had opened a kind of dark door within her. So many questions to be answered. Had the board spirits been real or just a figment of the imagination? In any case, she had to stop thinking of it now.

Mrs. Lilac pulled her sweater tightly around her. It was growing quite chilly, and the wind was blowing the brittle leaves into her face. Huge drops of rain fell from the sky at intervals. And suddenly, the only place she wanted to be, away from spirits, goblins, and the dark where they seemed to thrive, was back in the warmth and safety of her own bed.

NOVEMBER

Perhaps November is a month for seeing, not only the stark shape of the landscape, but the dark shapes of feelings and memories that lie deep in the mind.

From Mrs. Lilac's Journal

November was Mrs. Lilac's least favorite month. She actually dreaded its arrival due to the fact that it had such a bad reputation as far as she was concerned. So many terrible things had happened to her over the years in this awful month. The memory of these held and encircled her, as she stood at the sitting room window on a November Monday morning.

Outside, rain was falling. It had been coming down steadily for the past three days. Already, Rainbow River was far over its banks. It stretched away into the meadow and was a dark brown color. Mrs. Lilac had no fear that it would come as high as the cottage since the meadow became a lake at times such as these. It was just that the rain and her emotions all went together into a muddle she wished she didn't have to deal with. The trees along the stream were black and stark in the rain. All the leaves were gone, and the vistas stretched and stretched away endlessly.

Yes, there was always such a sadness in November. And loss. Her mother many years ago, and her father, and her darling Shing, all gone into the folds of November. And Danny. Usually she could bury that far away from her, but every year at this time, she relived the grief of his death. Her only child, gone at the age of 16 months, of pneumonia. And it brought back the terrible years in Altoona, and a husband who she had tried to rescue from the pits of alcohol and drug addiction, until Danny's death when she realized that the only person she could rescue was herself. And that's when she had come here to Caronsburg.

Mrs. Lilac sat down in the wicker chair by the window. She took a tissue from the box on the stand and dabbed at her eyes. So many times she had

50

asked God why she had had so much pain and suffering in her life, and always, she had been answered by some simple thing placed in her sight, such as the bright bloom of the geranium there by the window, or the sound of birdsong from somewhere. This morning, it came from Stormy jumping into her lap and actually kissing her on the tip of her nose. It made her see that no matter how much pain one had to face, there was joy in living. And perhaps it took a little extra time and understanding to realize it was the simple things in life that mattered most of all. And the final answer was, of course, that she had been placed on the earth to help others.

And the only way to deal with November was to live it day by day. So Mrs. Lilac took stock of things. Let the rain pound on the roof and let the wind sweep toward her across the meadow. Inside the cottage, she would make things as cozy as she could. She'd bake a cake and perhaps do a bit of cleaning before her first client arrived at one o'clock.

Mrs. Lilac had pretty much gotten her world a little more organized, both physically and emotionally, by the time the knock came at the door. As she went to answer it, she looked down and saw she was still dressed in her slacks and gray sweatshirt. But what did it matter. Take me as I am, she thought, or don't come at all.

She opened the door. It was a young woman, someone she'd never read for before. Somewhere in her thirties, she wore glasses and a bright smile. She had on a rain coat, but her short hair was neat and her makeup was impeccable, in spite of the rain.

I"m Twila Marchand," she said, holding out her hand.

"And I'm Mrs. Lilac, won't you come in?"

Mrs. Lilac took the girl's coat, and when they were comfortably seated at the table, Mrs. Lilac realized that this was someone she liked. She wasn't sure how she knew these things, but she did. As, many times during her readings, she wasn't sure where all the information came from. Oh, of course the cards were the pointers, but sometimes they opened vistas that surprised her.

"I somehow feel you have a relationship problem you'd like to discuss with me," Mrs. Lilac said, handing her the deck of cards.

"Yes, I do have a problem, and I think it best if I tell you something of it first. When you read the cards I want you to have all the information I can give you. I feel that's the best way."

"Yes it is," said Mrs. Lilac. "But you'd be surprised how many people want to test me, want me to come up with every detail, even things that no living man or woman could find or know. Some people think someone like myself knows everything of their past, present and future, and all I have to do is look at them and presto, there it is."

They laughed together, and Mrs. Lilac knew they would get along famously.

"It's my boyfriend," Mrs. Lilac. "I've been seeing him for three years. We met at the medical center where I work. I'm a physical therapist and he's a successful doctor. But there's a problem. He's married. He's promised me from the beginning that he would eventually leave his wife and we'd be married ourselves someday. But he has two small children, and he has not made any preparations for leaving. When I ask him anything at all, he tells me I must trust him and that I have to be patient." She stopped and twisted a small ring on her left hand. Her eyes dropped and her face took on a sad look. Finally, she looked up into Mrs. Lilac's gaze.

"But I don't feel right about the whole thing anymore. I feel intense guilt. All around me, friends and other people seem to be leading happy lives, getting married and having children, and I'm getting nowhere, having to hide every thing I'm doing, having to live a life of secrets. It's more than I can handle sometimes. And recently, I'm questioning if I love him at all. Mrs. Lilac, I need your advice."

"I understand your plight, dear," Mrs. Lilac told her. "But lets consult the cards now. Shuffle them well and we'll take a look. What are your sun signs?"

"I'm a Scorpio and he is Gemini."

"Not the best match under normal circumstances." Mrs Lilac said, as Twila shuffled the cards.

"You seem to be a rescuer in a way, perhaps you have a hard time seeing negative in anyone. But he is the type who very easily can have two women in his life. My husband was a Gemini, so perhaps I have a prejudice against him already."

Mrs. Lilac began laying down the cards. "I see how frustrating this has become for you," she said. "You have a desire to walk away from the whole thing. You are even willing to go to some unknown place, either real or imaginary, to free yourself from the anxiety you feel over this at times."

"I feel exactly like that, Mrs. Lilac," Twila said. "I'm actually having panic attacks where my heart races and I feel like I'm going crazy. And the worst thing is, we never get to go anywhere or do anything like a normal couple does. I feel I'm the mistress, but without the perks!"

"I don't think he will ever leave his wife, honey. I think he will go on like this forever. If not with you, then with someone else. There are too many indications in the cards that he is able to separate his two lives and has no intention of leaving his wife for you."

Twila began crying silently, trying to wipe the tears away with her hands. Mrs. Lilac handed her a tissue from the box beside her.

"I knew that's the way it was," Mrs. Lilac, "I just needed some confirmation that I wasn't crazy. He always makes it out that all my fears are unfounded and that if I wait just a little longer we will be together in the end. But how can I stop this? It's like a terrible habit I can't break!"

"Let me suggest something," Mrs. Lilac said after a moment of thought. "Your cards hold little hope for this relationship if it continues the way it is going. You will surely split up at some time in the future. You will reach the end of your rope. Either that or it will break, and that makes me afraid for you. You seem to be headed for some sort of a breakdown, as I see it.

Give him an ultimatum. What can you lose? Let him know he has to make a choice now, not ten years from now. Tell him you want truth and not promises. You will be better in the end, no matter what happens. At least it will be you who has made the decision."

Twila continued to cry and wipe at her eyes. Mrs. Lilac felt suddenly she was only a woman, not a reader, and the cards she had laid down were only paper. She found tears rolling down her own cheeks, suddenly.

"Things never change, dear," she said sadly. "We all have these moments where we have to make decisions that are crucial, if there is to be any happiness for us at all in life. I had something like this once myself. Oh, it was different but still the same decision, the same choice, happiness or destruction. I was married to a man who was an abusive alcoholic, and I stayed, year after year, believing I could somehow change the whole thing. In the end, we had a child, a little boy, and he died before he was two. My whole world fell down around me then. I hated my husband when he showed no emotion over losing his son. That was the final straw for me."

Mrs. Lilac suddenly realized she had crossed a line she tried very hard not to cross. She had actually spoken to a client about her own personal life. But she liked this young lady. Perhaps it would help her to know others suffered every day in the same way. And besides, it was November. Cold, heartless November, who, like a cold hearted man, took and took until there was nothing left to take.

There was silence for a long moment between them. Then Mrs. Lilac went to the other side of the table and gave the young woman a hug.

"There is a new life for you," she said. "One in which you can be your own person and hold your head high every time you step out the door. I had a chance for a new life once myself, and I took it. After my divorce, I left Altoona and moved here to Caronsburg and rebuilt my life from the ashes.

And the cards showed me another thing, that there will be someone else for you when you are ready for him to come in. It's all up to you."

When the girl had finally asked her last question, hugged her and was gone, Mrs. Lilac felt that she had made a new friend. She was always able to tell when someone would come to see her again, and she knew that this one would.

The rain finally stopped and the cold crept in. The November sun was cold and harsh. Mrs. Lilac stayed close to the house. The walks were short and right to the point. Rainbow River shrank back to its normal size, and Mrs. Lilac resigned herself to the fact that winter was here and would have to be dealt with, one day at a time.

On a dark Thursday evening after the readings, she put on one of her warmest coats and took Scrappy on his leash down to the stream. A full moon rose above the meadow, huge and bright. It seemed a deeper, darker color than normal. And she thought of a line from a poem she had written once, "Moon you are a blind Gypsy, the sun is your lamp."

Staring at the moon, she seemed to reflect on all that had happened to her over the past few months. It seemed the full moon usually had an effect on people, but with her it always seemed to make her look deep within herself. It made her remember the past, people who had played out their time on the stage of her life. And of course, there was always the sense of sadness and loss. But tonight, somehow, she was surprised by the slight feeling of hope that lay at the bottom of what she was thinking. But where was it coming from? She still had no idea where she would go when her lease was up in May. She had spoken not a word with Mr. Gately. But somehow, there in the November moonlight, she felt a tinge of hope. It surprised her, shocked her a bit, but the feeling buoyed her, and her steps seemed easier as she headed back to the house.

But she should have been wary of any such hopefulness. November was a trickster. He opened a door and slammed it shut. Just when you thought you saw a clear path ahead, November reduced it to shadows. She was no sooner in the door than the phone rang.

"Mrs. Lilac, this is Jill Brady, do you remember me?"

Mrs. Lilac was caught off guard. "Oh, yes," she remembered. "You're Patty's daughter. I haven't heard from her lately."

"I"m sorry, Mrs. Lilac. Mother died last week. I should have called you sooner. But it was a shock, and there was so much to see to and do."

Mrs. Lilac had to sit down. Her heart seemed to stop momentarily. Patty had been one of her first clients. How many years ago?

"Mother always thought so highly of you, Mrs. Lilac. She always told me if it weren't for you, she couldn't have gotten through the divorce from my father."

"Yes, she often told me that too," Mrs. Lilac said, trying to compose herself.

"But I will always feel guilt that I couldn't have foreseen the cancer."

"Don't blame yourself," Mrs. Lilac. "Mother never wanted to accept that there was anything really wrong."

"I know," Mrs. Lilac replied sadly, "I remember the day she told me she had found the lump. I told her she should see her doctor. But she told me she didn't have health insurance. I should have insisted. Yet, like so many people, it was easier for her to just ignore it than to face what it might be. But I will never forget your mother. We had so many laughs together. It was always a joy to see her."

Later, Mrs. Lilac reflected on many things. She sat silently on the sofa until after midnight thinking of life and her purpose in it. The pets got tired waiting for her to go to bed and went without her. The house was still as death, and the awful November moonlight streamed in.

"You are not God," the voice of the unconscious spoke to her through the ears of her soul. "You cannot wave your wand and make everything perfect for everyone. You are only one woman and must learn lessons also as you grow. Believe in yourself and accept what joy you find in being alive."

It was hard, she realized, knowing she couldn't have done more to save her friend, but she had to accept the fact that each person alive on the earth is in charge of his own destiny. She said a silent prayer then for her friend Patty. She knew she was in a better world, one of happiness and light. She had to believe that.

She finally was able to go to bed and she did sleep, and when she woke the next morning, things seemed a bit improved. The sun shone in the window, and looking out, she saw it would be a cold day. There was frost all across the meadow, and the stream looked icy cold. Her inner weather seemed a bit better as well. The sadness was there, but it seemed less painful, after the night's rest. Perhaps the effect of the full moon had reached a kind of high point, just as the tides of the ocean along the shore. And now she felt that she could bear and deal with anything that came along.

The walk with the pets was quick and short, and as it was Friday and shopping day, she sat writing a list at the table while she had her coffee. Perhaps getting away from the house might give her another kind of lift.

She was nearly finished with her coffee when the phone rang.

"Mrs. Lilac?" A female voice said when she answered, "This is Joanne

Barkely. We met at Goldie's house, at the Halloween party. I am the Feather Lady."

"Oh yes of course," Mrs. Lilac said. "I remember you."

"Well, I'm sorry to bother you, but I would like to come see you, perhaps sometime tomorrow. I want to bring my daughter. I should have spoken to you that night, but the board reading shocked me so badly, I had to be away from there. You see, my daughter was a friend of a girl named Becky Wilson. She was hit by a car last year and killed. I don't know if that was who came through on the board that night or not. It spelled out Rebecca, and that was Becky's given name, though she never used it. But anyway, her death was kind of mysterious, and I would like to talk to you about it."

"Well, I think I could see you, tomorrow," Mrs. Lilac said, trying to remember her schedule. "Perhaps around one o'clock. Would that work?"

"Great," said Mrs. Barkely. "We'll be there."

After she'd hung up the phone, Mrs. Lilac thought back to the night of the party. The Feather Lady had been out of there in a hurry, and no one seemed willing to talk about the session with the Ouija board. She didn't, herself, take much stock in anything it had spelled out that night. Both she and Fern had sat for the session just to please the hostess, and it had tired them both and made them uncomfortable, both that and the idea of the place being haunted. For someone who dealt with looking into the future, Mrs. Lilac was a person with both feet planted firmly on the ground. She believed in the spirit world. She believed there was a beautiful place where everyone went home to when they passed out of this life, but she also believed in living one life at a time. She believed in telling the truth and never tried to pull the wool over anyone's eyes. Fooling someone with the Ouija board was just not her idea of a good thing. She was just not sure how it operated. Was it the subconscious working? Was it a spirit? She knew that on the night in question, though her hands were on the pointer along with Fern's, she was as surprised as anyone else when it started to spell out letters, words and sentences. Perhaps the session with the Feather Lady and her daughter would shed some light on what had happened.

Out of the feather outfit, and dressed in jeans and a light blue sweater, the Feather Lady looked like any other forty-year-old woman. She was quite attractive with long brown hair and a smooth complexion. Her daughter was almost a carbon copy of her mother, except that her hair was shorter and she was naturally a teenager. She also wore jeans, a cute green top and a tan jacket. They arrived precisely at one the following afternoon. Mrs. Lilac brought an extra chair to the table and then took her usual place at the end.

56

"You look different without the feathers," Mrs. Lilac said with a small laugh. "I did think your costume was quite original, and I was impressed by what you do for young people".

"Oh, thank you Mrs. Lilac." Joanne said. "I try very hard to make a difference."

"By the way, this is my daughter, Trina. She's a senior this year at the high school, and she wants to be a nurse also when she's finished with her schooling."

Trina was a bit shy and ill at ease, as though she didn't know what to expect. She rubbed her hands together and fussed with a small stone ring on her left hand.

"First of all," said Mrs. Lilac, "I want you to know that what happened with the board that night was entirely automatic. Neither myself or my friend were doing anything to move the pointer. I have no idea how the board works, but the Ouija board has a long history. One interesting note is that years ago, in St. Louis, a spirit by the name of Patience Worth came through a board that was operated by two women there. Patience spelled out many messages and even wrote novels, among other things. One, in fact, was called "The Sorry Tale", and was about Christ. So I won't be able to explain why the board said what it said that night or why those two entities came through. But if you think I can help with anything that is worrying you, I will certainly be willing to try."

"I'll let my daughter tell you about what happened to her friend Becky, and then perhaps you'll understand why I was so upset that night."

Trina lowered her eyes and then began to speak, slowly at first and then with more confidence and animation.

"Becky and I were friends since grade school," she said. "We told each other everything. We were planning to go to the same college. Becky was a cheerleader, and her boyfriend, Scott, played basketball. The night she died, about two years ago, they had both been at a game, and Scott was taking her home. He was really tired, so to get him home faster, Becky insisted he just drop her at the end of her street. She actually lived on a township road, one that had no streetlights or sidewalks. Their house was about a quarter of a mile further along. When she didn't show up at home, her mother called Scott's house, and he told her he had dropped her at the end of the road over an hour before." Trina began to cry suddenly, and her voice broke. Mrs. Lilac handed her a wad of tissues. After a moment, she went on.

"Her mother got in the car and headed down the road. She came across Becky's body, lying not far from the cross street, right on the edge of the macadam. By the time she was able to get an ambulance, Becky was dead."

57

"How awful for her," Mrs. Lilac said. "What a terrible tragedy."

"Yes," said Joanne, taking up the story. Trina's face was buried in her hands and tissues. "And the worst part is, they never found out what happened. It was obvious she had been struck by a car, but no one came forward, of course. And many people wanted to turn a suspicious eye on Scott, and it just devastated him. He's never been the same. We have all tried to put it behind us, but without closure, as far as knowing who did this to her, it's just so hard. You can imagine how I felt when Rebecca came through the board that night."

"I know exactly how you must have felt," Mrs. Lilac said. "A terrible tragedy in any case, but even worse when it happens to someone close to you."

"Do you have any ideas, Mrs. Lilac? Do you suppose it could have been Becky coming through the board? Do you think she wanted to tell us something?"

"I'm not going to say it was her," Mrs. Lilac said. "Sometimes thinking we have communicated with the dead brings comfort, but I also will not say it was not. Rebecca is a fairly common name. But the board did say she was killed. I can often can pick out the dead in the cards. And I totally believe in life after death and the other side. However, I believe that when we pass into that realm, we no longer think as humans think. Often we who are left search for a message from the loved one, and the only message is a simple one, a message of love. I think we should lay out a spread of cards on the girl's death and see if there is anything to be gleaned from them."

Mrs. Barkely nodded and Mrs. Lilac handed her the cards. Mrs. Lilac suggested that both she and her daughter take turns shuffling them.

When they were finished, Mrs. Lilac started laying them out on the table.

"The cards are very dark," Mrs. Lilac began, "but then it was a dark night obviously, and the car that hit your friend was speeding. It seemed to have happened so fast it couldn't have been prevented. And Becky obviously didn't have time to think about stepping aside."

"The cards show panic, fear, extreme anxiety. It was hit and run, and it looks like the person responsible, still suffers from his or her guilt."

"I do think, however, that there is a real chance that this case will eventually be solved. The cards of the future are bright. Here we have the Sun and the World, and it looks like Justice will prevail in the end."

"Do you think Becky is happy where she is, Mrs. Lilac?" Trina asked, her face still wet with tears. "I try to think of her that way."

"I'm sure she's happy, my dear. She's in a world of peace and contentment, and she says we should not mourn for her. You see, when we go to that place, we know we are home. Earth cannot compare to a world that is so beautiful, no human can ever describe it."

"But you must believe me that the truth will come out in this situation. I see a dark night, but I also see the dawn. I see fear and then I see relief and peace. I have no idea who could have been driving that car, but I feel almost certain that we will know someday, and perhaps sooner than we think. And, as I said, if it were your friend coming through on the board that night, perhaps her simple message might have been, "I am still alive. I am still here, and I love you."

Mrs. Lilac felt so helpless at times, and this moment was one of them. There was so much she wanted to give, so much she knew she couldn't. And even the smallest comfort came at a high cost to her own sense of purpose. But Joanne and her daughter seemed satisfied with what she was able to tell them. They stayed awhile longer and asked several more questions, but finally left her alone.

Afterwards, she sat there on the sofa for a long moment. She shook her head. There was too much suffering in the world, and each day it seemed to get worse.

She finally put on her coat and took the animals out into the bright afternoon for their walk. There was a sharp nip to the air and the wind was blowing. A jaunt through the junk yard still made a pleasant walk, though her thoughts were jumbled and it was hard to concentrate on the joy of the moment. Even Scrappy's dancing at her feet and loud barking at a scurrying rabbit, failed to get her mind in focus. Stormy did his usual disappearing trick, and they had made the entire circle before he suddenly came from behind a hulking piece of machinery to rejoin them at the end.

Back at the house, she was just getting ready to go in the door when she heard a car behind her in the driveway. Scrappy barked excitedly. She turned and, with a slight skip to her heartbeat, saw that it was Bill Green. He carried another basket of apples in one hand and a large pumpkin in the other. Her pie pan was held precariously under his left arm. He wore a heavy coat and brown pants. There was a sheepish grin on his face.

"I brought back your pan," he said. "The pie was delicious. I haven't had pie like that since my wife died."

Mrs. Lilac reached out and took the pan from under his arm, and saw that the mention of his wife took the grin from his face. But it was soon back. "So I thought I'd bring more apples. Perhaps..."

"Perhaps I might bake you another? Why I'd be happy too."

"And," he said," with a laugh, "I wonder if you do pumpkin as well."

59

"You know, my mother was the pumpkin pie baker," she told him, as she took his coat and motioned him to the sofa. "Her pies were so delicious they were indescribable. When she died, she left no recipe, so I have spent years trying to get one to taste like hers. I come close but just don't quite make it. But that is a nice pumpkin you've brought, so perhaps I can try again."

She made a fresh pot of coffee and served it to him in an extra large mug. There was also a large piece of her best coconut cake to go with it, and she could tell by the way he ate it that he enjoyed it immensely.

"This is delicious cake," he said, shaking his head. "These days, I'm used to the store bought kind. I've even got on to cooking for myself a little. I can do a fried chicken that isn't half bad, and eggs and more eggs in a dozen different ways. So, I get by."

"So how have you been feeling lately," Mrs. Lilac asked, "Is it getting any better?"

"You know, I have to say there does seem to be a weight lifted from my shoulders, Mrs. Barnes."

"Please call me Betty," she interrupted. "I'd like that."

"Okay, then I'm Bill," he went on. "I still have my sad days, but I keep thinking about the things you told me that first day I was here. You seem to have a wisdom about you that isn't of this world. You seem like you are able to lift above things to see them in a different way."

"Oh, I don't know," she said. "I do what I can do. I just see that you have so much left to give and to do. You obviously have a good heart and you just have to keep walking through this country of grief you find yourself in. The path will lead you to the other side of the trees one day. Believe me, I know what I'm saying."

After he'd drank another cup of coffee, he stood up and prepared to leave.

She handed him his coat, and before he put it on, he lowered his eyes and reached out and gave her a quick hug.

Mrs. Lilac was taken a bit aback. He smelled like the earth, warm, alive. His arms were so strong, and she was sorry when he dropped them and stepped back.

"I'll bake you a pie," she told him. "Better still, why don't you come to dinner, maybe in December, closer to Christmas? I'll lay a nice holiday spread out for us, and I'll serve you pumpkin pie, as much like my mother's as I can make it."

"I'd like that very much," he said. "Just give me a ring to set up the date. I'm in the book."

After he was gone, Mrs. Lilac stood holding onto the door knob. It seemed to her, for a moment, that she would fall, her heart was beating so fast. She had tried to stop thinking of him in that female, human way. She was too far along in her life to believe that anything special could come of a friendship with a gentleman, especially one who was obviously still grieving for his wife. But today the circle of joy had come closer and not further away. So close, in fact, she felt as though it were holding her with a rope of kindness that she might never be able to let go of.

November was such a terrible expanse, but from the joyful feeling inside her, she knew its awful journey was nearing an end. The new month lay before her like a promise. In her mind, she imagined she saw starlight shining over snow.

DECEMBER

One has to be careful now with memory. December has a way of making our yesterdays more or less than what they really were. It brightens, darkens, enlarges or shrinks any bit of reality until it becomes its own phenomena, a brightly wrapped moment to keep.

From Mrs. Lilac's Journal

One December morning, Mrs. Lilac looked out the bedroom window and beheld a fairyland. There had been a light rain during the night, and it had all turned to ice. The trees and bushes along the creek bank were all encapsulated with a thin layer of crystal. It was like the picture on an old fashioned Christmas card, but as beautiful as it was, by the time she was up and about and had taken Scrappy out for his morning walk, it was already melting. Bits of ice were falling everywhere, from the trees and bushes, from the corners of the cottage. The sounds the pieces of crystal made as they fell were like music from a delicate wind chime.

Christmas was everywhere, in the air, in the cottage, in her head, in the town. Christmas day would be spent at home, a quiet lunch with Fern. But there were many things to be done. A lot of baking, because she always liked to give cookies to her clients. And she was already crocheting in any spare moment she had. There was a large afghan she was making for Fern, some mittens for the homeless shelter, and a possible gift of a scarf for Bill Green to wear around his neck.

Mrs. Lilac tried to keep her Christmases as simple as possible. Elaborate gifts were not for her. Something you made with your hands, was the perfect way of showing someone you cared for, that they were special. And Mrs. Lilac enjoyed sending and receiving Christmas cards. She liked the ones that made her remember the early years of her life, the happiest years of all, which she had spent with her parents in the country. She was the only child and they were quite poor, but her mother was an extremely creative woman. She had made miracles from bits of promise. Those simple Christmases were the kind she tried to have in her own home.

And then, of course, in her mind, she had been going over the preparations for her special holiday dinner for Bill Green. She had already called him on the phone and set Saturday, the fifteenth, as the date for the get-together. He was pleased with that, from what she could tell from his voice.

Despite all the preparations for the holiday, there were still the clients, and she was surprised at how many people seemed to want to come see her at this time of year. But then she knew from past experience, that if our expectations are too high, the holidays can be disastrous and depressing.

On this particular morning, her first client was Nancy, the girl she had seen in the summer, the girl who whispered and was afraid of totally losing her voice.

This time, when Mrs. Lilac met her at the door, she was shocked when the girl said, "Mrs. Lilac, how are you?" Her voice was normal and natural in tone and volume.

"Oh, Nancy, listen to you. What has happened?"

"I"m well again, Mrs. Lilac! And this is for you." She handed Mrs. Lilac a small package wrapped in bright red foil.

When they were seated at the table, Nancy was so animated and had so much to say, Mrs. Lilac could barely get a word in.

"I did what you told me to do, Mrs. Lilac. I talked to my doctor and told him he had to send me to someone else. I told him I knew there was someone out there who could help me. He finally did some research, made some calls, and sent me to a specialist in Pittsburgh. He was a wonderful man, and he knew exactly what needed to be done. It was some kind of shock therapy. He applied it to my vocal cords and after a few treatments, here I am."

"Oh, Nancy, what a wonderful thing for you!"

"But Mrs. Lilac," Nancy was very serious suddenly, "you must take some credit for my healing. If it hadn't been for you, I probably would have just accepted that I would spend the rest of my life with no voice. You encouraged me, gave me hope. You are an angel, Mrs. Lilac, and that little gift I brought you will always remind you of that. Now please open your package."

Mrs. Lilac had set the small gift on the table beside her, and she picked it up and delicately unwrapped it. She was not good about receiving gifts. She never felt she was as worthy as the giver always felt she was. When the paper was off and the small box was opened, she found a delicate crystal angel lying inside. She was totally complete, from the tips of her wings to the top of her halo.

"Oh, how beautiful," Mrs. Lilac cried. She took the angel from the box and set it in the center of the table. "I do appreciate your thoughtfulness. I just don't believe I had an awful lot to do with your recovery. I just gave you a little advice."

"You gave me more than that, Mrs. Lilac. You've given me my life again. And the best news is, I'm pregnant! Yes, while I was going through my problem, I didn't think my marriage would survive. I became quite self centered, and my husband felt as though I was pushing him away. And now, since I'm well again, we've become closer and have something positive to look forward to. You are an angel, truly you are, Mrs. Lilac."

When the girl was gone, Mrs. Lilac sat at the table for a moment in reflection. She dabbed at her eyes with a tissue. It always made her feel so good to hear that someone had overcome an obstacle, had stepped up to the plate and hit a home run. She never wanted to believe that she had said or done anything that was anymore than she was meant to do or say. She was just a simple woman and was never able to figure out why people wanted to put her on a pedestal.

December sped up as it always did. One morning, she looked out the window and snow was falling. It came down fast, and the next thing she knew, several inches had accumulated and the phone began to ring and appointments were canceled. It was a beautiful snowfall, the kind that layered and tufted on trees and bushes, the meadow looked like a magical expanse as it faded into a misty white.

She took Scrappy outside and set him free from his lease. He went crazy in the snow, rolling in it, running in circles, and rushed down to the stream where bits of snow dropped from the trees onto the surface of the dark water. Stormy hated snow, didn't like to get his feet wet, so he watched them from the window, his eyes wide with wonder. She imagined Shing was sitting there beside him. For Shing had also hated snow and sometimes would not emerge from the house for days until most of the hated stuff melted.

In the late afternoon, David showed up in the pickup truck. He was dressed like a snowman, and had brought his shovels to dig her out. By this time, the snow had slacked and the air had turned colder. Mrs. Lilac made fresh coffee and set out a plate of cookies for her guest. When he came in finally, breathless, his cheeks were red and he had a big smile on his face.

"Got you shoveled out Mrs. Barnes," he said. "Snow's great, isn't it?"

"It's beautiful, at least. How are things going for you, David? School going okay?"

"Great, it's all great. I'm all set for college in the Fall."

When she'd given him coffee and his cookies, she suddenly remembered Becky, the girl who died. Perhaps David had known her.

"David, did you know Becky, the girl who was killed in the hit and run a couple of years ago? One of her friends was here and told me about it."

"I knew her vaguely, Mrs. Barnes, I saw her from time to time in the hall and all. We didn't have any classes together."

"Were there any theories at the time about how it happened?"

"The guys talked a little. Probably someone from Mountain Green Tavern taking a short cut, drunk and going too fast. The bar is out there on the township road. The short cut to town goes past where she lived."

Mrs. Lilac lowered her eyes and took a sip of her coffee.

"I hear you baked Bill Green an apple pie." She looked up and saw the sheepish look on David's face. His lips curled in a kind of grin. "He said it was quite good, too."

Mrs. Lilac felt color rush to her cheeks. She was totally at a loss for words.

"I didn't mean to embarrass you, Mrs. Barnes." David said, quietly. "You really must have helped him, you know. But from the way he acted when he talked about you, I think he likes you a bit, too."

"Oh, that can't be," she said, breathing hard.

"Why not, Mrs. Barnes? You are a wonderful woman. Why is it so unusual that someone would like you? Like that, I mean."

"Like what?"

"Like a man, woman thing, you know. You're single and available. He's a widower. You know, talk, date, that sort of thing."

Mrs. Lilac was speechless. She pushed the plate of cookies toward her guest. Maybe if he ate more, he wouldn't talk so much.

A couple of days later, she went into Caronsburg for her usual ramble around the town circle with her friend, Fern. It was after six o'clock, and everywhere she looked, Christmas shone out across the night. Fern lived in a kind of gingerbread house out near the end of Main Street. She had a huge garage in the back that she used for a studio. Both the house and studio were extremely cluttered, but the whole place had a certain charm, and Mrs. Lilac enjoyed visiting, though there wasn't much time for their get-togethers.

Fern was glad to see her. She was dressed in a red and green sweater with a large wreath pin. Mrs. Lilac was also dressed in a sweater, bright red over a pair of warm, dark slacks. The air was chilly, but it was a clear night. A lot of the snow was still in place, but the streets and sidewalks had been cleared.

"Let's have a cup of hot tea before we venture out," Fern said. She laid out the tea cups and some thinly sliced fruitcake. "We'll have another cup down at the Grill, after we've seen the circle, but for now lets just get ourselves warmed up. I have a surprise for you. I'll let you know what it is when we get back."

The walk downtown was lovely. The town converged in a circle, and all around it were small shops, all decorated for the holidays. A huge tree had been placed in the small green park at the center, and right in front of it was a lovely creche, one of the most beautiful Mrs. Lilac had ever seen. Mrs. Lilac had spent many years working there on the circle. She had worked in the Tri Point Pharmacy until it closed. And she had met many people while working there. That's how she had first become friends with Fern. So it was always good to come back to it. The shop windows were so bright and colorful, and there were the bell ringers and the sound of carols being sung from the huge Methodist church as they passed. Surprisingly, there were very few people out this evening. The larger shopping mall at the edge of town had caused a loss of business for the local merchants. The Grill was also not very busy as they went inside. They found a small table at the back, and a waitress served them tea in no time at all.

While they sat there, Mrs. Lilac noticed two women at a table near the front. Both were somewhere in their fifties with graying hair. One was thin, the other, a little more matronly. They were looking in her direction, and she noticed them whispering and staring at her. Fern seemed not to notice. She was rambling on and on about this or that and was lost somewhere among the words.

Mrs. Lilac felt quite uncomfortable, because she knew by the looks on their faces that the two women were talking about her being the local witch, or whatever such thing they wanted to call her. This had happened to her before, so she easily caught the drift of what was going on. Finally, she and Fern were done with their tea and went out of the place. The two ladies were dead silent as they passed their table. But when they had stepped outside, Mrs. Lilac turned and looked back. The two of them were still staring at her, and she could feel the coldness like a knife.

Back at her home, Fern bustled about and finally went into another room and brought out a flat package about a foot square, wrapped in plain brown paper.

This is your Christmas gift," she said, excitedly. "I couldn't wait until Christmas to give it to you. Please open it. I can't wait until you see what it is."

Mrs. Lilac tore the paper from the package and immediately burst into tears. It was a portrait of Shing. She sat, a lovely tiger cat, on the window sill.

She looked directly into Mrs. Lilac's heart. Behind her, she was also reflected in the glass. The curtains were bright blue, and in the background were lovely tones of blue and green. The frame was of barn wood, rustic and just right.

She was speechless and tears continued to fall. Fern never failed to surprise her. Dotty as she was, Fern always seemed to know what she was thinking and what would please her. She remembered that once she had mentioned something to Fern about painting Shing, but you never knew if Fern heard anything you said or even paid attention to any of it. But she must have heard. She always seemed to get it right in the end.

"Do you like it?" Fern asked, offering her a tissue.

Mrs. Lilac couldn't speak. She was only able to nod her head.

The fifteenth dawned cold and clear. Mrs. Lilac went through the house making sure everything was perfect for her guest. She had put up her small tree the day before. It looked so festive there on the stand by the window. It was dressed in homemade wood ornaments, and colorful miniature lights. A perfect star topped the whole thing off. She put a bright red cloth over the table in the living room, and had already set it with her best blue willow plates. The centerpiece was one that she used year after year. A large reindeer surrounded by artificial pine and mistletoe.

The menu she had planned was for a baked ham, sweet potatoes and all the trimmings, including homemade coleslaw and hot rolls. She had baked two kinds of pie, apple and pumpkin. Two of them, one of each, were gifts for her guest. The house smelled like a bakery, and the animals wanted to live in the kitchen; they had been given so many small morsels of this or that.

She played Christmas carols on the radio as she continued her preparations, and from time to time, she would go into her bedroom and look at Fern's portrait of Shing. She had hung it right by the window, Shing's favorite window, the one that she had used as an entrance and exit, at anytime of the day or night. Mrs. Lilac had always kept the window up and the screen slid to the side slightly, giving her just enough space, but then one day she had brought in a baby rabbit, and Mrs. Lilac had had to spend an hour chasing the creature around the house. After that, Mrs. Lilac became the doorkeeper. Sad as it was to remember, especially at Christmas when everything was meant to be filled with joy and light, the portrait gave her a comforting feeling, a feeling of time remembered, of something warm and beautiful, always there in a corner of her heart.

Her guest arrived precisely at six o'clock. Mrs. Lilac felt weak and spaced out, just seeing him there in the doorway. It looked as though the slacks and gray sweater he wore, under a thick winter coat, were the very best he had.

He had brought her a huge basket of poinsettia, both red and white blossoms, and Mrs. Lilac made room for it on her Mother's oak buffet that sat along the one wall of the living room.

"They're beautiful," she told him. "You couldn't have brought me anything nicer."

"I thought of bringing you a tree from the farm," he said, "but figured you probably already had one. But there's always next year."

"Next year," she thought, hanging up his coat. "Will I even survive this dinner?"

But they finally sat down at the table, and Mrs. Lilac was soon herself again. Serving the food helped. And while she didn't think of herself as the world's best cook, she had a kind of confidence when she was preparing and offering it to others. She was not afraid of anything to do with the meal itself, only that she might embarrass herself in front of this gentleman who had opened doorways into her feelings that she hadn't even realized were there.

The meal went beautifully. The two candles she had lit on either side of her reindeer, gave the whole table a festive glow. The food was delicious, even if she had to say so herself, and Bill Green heartily agreed and had two helpings of everything. Mrs. Lilac offered a mild chilled red wine in crystal glasses, and there was the pumpkin pie for dessert. Bill Green ate the pie as though it were the most delicious he'd ever eaten, and even her own taste buds came alive with the fond memory of her mother's face, looking on with approval.

Bill Green sat quietly on the sofa while Mrs. Lilac, after declining his help, cleared the table.

The Christmas music continued to play in the background, and Mrs. Lilac couldn't remember when she had felt so happy. She was dizzy really, perhaps a bit from the wine, perhaps from the excitement, but mostly it was because Bill Green was sitting right there on the sofa with her two pets, one on either side of him. Stormy loved the attention, and Scrappy was lying on his back, all four feet in the air, his head hanging over the edge of the sofa.

When the table was cleared, Mrs. Lilac sat on the chair opposite and listened while Bill talked about his dairy farm operation, and of his children and grandson. Eventually the conversation turned to his wife.

"I'm beginning to accept it, truly I am." he said. There's not as much guilt, and I'm a bit used to fending for myself. I realize now, I was quite a bit of a workaholic, but if she minded, she never showed it. She was just always there when I came in at night. It was comforting. That I still miss."

"Time takes care of everything in the end," Mrs. Lilac said. "No matter how awful or horrible the event or loss, we go on in spite of ourselves."

"Yes, I realize that," he went on. "I have started to look ahead, even make plans without feeling guilty. She wouldn't want me to be unhappy. She told me once when she was so sick that I should try to go on with my life, but I was so caught up in the way I felt, my concern for her, that I didn't even let it register."

This time when he was ready to leave, the hug was a bit longer. Mrs. Lilac heard a catch to his breath in that brief instant before he let her go, but she recognized it as a kind of sigh, for all he had lost, and perhaps too, that he had actually looked down the road of the future, and decided it was the only way to go.

Before he put on his coat, Mrs. Lilac brought out the scarf she had crocheted for him. She had done it in two shades of blue. She placed it around his neck.

"I've made a little something for you," she said. "I hope it keeps you a bit warmer through these cold days."

He seemed a bit taken aback, but he thanked her and ran his hand across its softness. It seemed as though he could find nothing else to say. Mrs. Lilac put on her own coat and walked with him to his truck. She carried the two pies she had baked for him. There was a moon, nearly full, over the snow, and the stars shone, actually blazed, above them.

"They say it takes an incredible number of years for that light to get to us," Bill Green said looking up at the sky.

Yes, I know," Mrs. Lilac said. "I wish we had that much time."

"So do I," he answered, "but we don't, believe me, we don't." He opened the truck door. "Thank you Betty," he said finally, after a short pause in which he continued to look up at the stars. "Thank you for a perfect evening. Everything was beautiful, including you. Merry Christmas."

She stepped back and the truck pulled out into the road. She followed it as far as she could with her eyes.

The days leading up to Christmas were warm, and much of the snow melted. Mrs. Lilac was a bit sad that there might not be any left for the holiday. By the morning of Christmas eve, she found a lot of things to be sad about, in fact. There were the usual things of course, but now that the worst of the holiday preparations were behind her, she had a lot more time for going back to the idea of having to move in the spring. She had tried not to think of the realization that this would be her last Christmas here in the cottage, but all during the past month, that nagging thought had been in the back of her mind. Her dinner for Bill Green had been a total success and had given her a rush of happiness and joy that she had not felt in a long time, but even that had fallen behind her in the build up of old concerns and fears.

So she was quite excited and happy when she had a phone call early that morning from her friends Wanda and Julie. They would be dropping by later that evening to bring her a bit of Christmas cheer. The two girls had been clients of hers for years. She had helped them get through the death of Wanda's sister, Kathy, a couple of years before, along with a dozen and one other concerns that usually plagued them. The duo had been friends since high school, and now, somewhere in there forties, they lived with Wanda's mother Florence, and their three Boston Terriers, Bo, Dixie and Odie.

The girls might as well have been twins. You never saw one of them without the other. Mrs. Lilac thought of them as Tweedle Dum and Tweedle Dee, though she never told them that and never thought of it in a mean way. She actually liked the girls, though their beliefs and interests were so different. The two of them had, over the years, delved into, and attached themselves to, every strange phenomena that came along. At the moment, they were deeply interested in Atlantis, ghosts, the hollow earth theory, big foot, alien abduction, Isis, and an upcoming shift in the earth's axis that would cause major catastrophes involving weather and temperatures. A couple of years before, during a summer picnic by the stream, Mrs. Lilac had made the mistake of mentioning her imaginary water goddess. The two of them had stared into the stream in awe, and now, each time they came, they would rush down to the water and throw in some kind of offering for the goddess, as Mrs. Lilac had often done. It might be a cookie, a stone, a bundle of sticks. Once, they dumped a large bottle of beer into the water. At times, Mrs. Lilac found the whole thing amusing, at others, she just shook her head and wondered what they would get into next. If nothing else, they gave her a good laugh. But that was okay, because the two of them were usually the ones who were laughing the loudest.

That evening, Mrs. Lilac lit candles and laid out fruit, cheese, crackers, cookies and a large vegetable tray. The girls were always on diets, though you could never tell that from looking at them. They were both well over the poundage of most dieters. Their latest interest was big Yoga for oversized girls. They went every Friday night and had often asked Mrs. Lilac to attend with them. She had always declined. Wanda was dark with short hair, and Julie was blond with hair that usually curled off in a hundred different directions. Wanda worked as a nurse, and Julie was a Veterinarian's assistant.

It was after eight when they arrived. Mrs. Lilac could hardly believe what she saw when she opened the door. Wanda wore a lighted Santa's cap that was playing Christmas carols. Julie wore a set of reindeer antlers that twinkled and played music at the same time. They were both dressed in fur coats over slacks and sweaters. Wanda had on a green sweater and red slacks and Julie wore just the opposite.

"Merry Christmas, Mrs. Lilac!" they cried together. And they stood there laughing like maniacs. Stormy flew into the bedroom, quite alarmed, and Scrappy's barking was more fierce than Mrs. Lilac had heard it for awhile. She also suddenly burst into laughter seeing them standing there like that, their arms full of an assorted mass of bags and packages.

They finally made it into the room, and after their coats and paraphernalia had been taken and laid down, they both tried talking at once. Mrs. Lilac had a hard time trying to take it all in.

"And as I was saying to Julie," Wanda said, "We've got to take some of our famous eggnog out to Mrs. Lilac. She needs to kick up her heels. The poor soul is always reading cards and doesn't get a moment of fun in her life."

"That's so true," Julie said. "And I told Wanda, she's simply going to overwork and fall over some day with a heart attack, and who will find her out there in that wilderness? Yes, she needs to jump out of that box."

"And wait until you see what I've brought you," Wanda, said, going through the assorted packages and bags on the floor. She finally pulled out a long box and handed it to Mrs. Lilac.

Mrs Lilac tore open the box and looked inside. It was a foot long magic wand. Down the length of the wand was written, Believe in Angels. There was a large star at the end. Each of the five points held a different word, joy, hope, peace, love and fun.

"Now, every time you finish reading cards," Julie said excitedly, "you tap your client five times on the shoulder with that for luck." They all laughed loudly, especially Mrs. Lilac, who found the thought particularly amusing.

"My gift is a little more practical," Julie said, handing Mrs. Lilac another package. It turned out to be crystal candle holders. The top was shaped like a star and the stem swirled downward to a gold base. There were also jingle bells, balls, and a large bag of treats for the pets.

Mrs. Lilac thanked them both sincerely, and gave each of them a matching scarf and pair of gloves she had crocheted. Then the girls dived into the food, and there was complete silence for a few moments while they sampled everything she had laid out. Wanda poured each of them a crystal glass of the eggnog she had brought in a large thermos.

"It's spiked, Mrs. Lilac." she said. "It'll warm your spirits on this cold night."

Mrs. Lilac took a large sip and it certainly was warming as it went down.

"And let's not forget the Water Goddess." Julie broke in. "Wait until you see what we've brought her." She reached into one of the bags and pulled out a large flat stone which she handed to Mrs. Lilac. It was actually made of an artificial resin. On the top of it was carved the word, Peace. She pulled out two more. One read Love, another Joy.

"Aren't these fabulous?" Wanda asked. "We found them in the garden center this summer. You are supposed to place them around your garden. But we're going to throw them into the stream for the goddess."

Mrs. Lilac couldn't help but shake her head. What would they think of next? But later, when they had their fill of the food, they all put on their coats and meandered down to the stream. Wanda insisted they bring their glasses and the rest of the egg nog along.

Mrs. Lilac took her largest flashlight, because it seemed very dark outside. The sky was overcast, and it was hard to see any stars, though they were visible from place to place if you looked closely enough. The air was sharp, but the wind was still. The creek made its own music as they stood there. Off across the meadow, there was a glow where the strips of snowy earth met the sky.

After they'd drank a toast of egg nog for health wealth and happiness, Mrs. Lilac insisted that they join hands and say a silent prayer to God for Peace on Earth. Then, one by one, they went up to the edge of the stream with their offering for the Goddess. Mrs Lilac threw in Peace, Wanda threw in Love and Julie threw in Joy. A loud splash sounded after each one, and then, once again, they stood silently looking up at the sky. Suddenly, a snowflake fell, and then another. Soon it was actually snowing, the flakes touching their upturned faces.

"Perfect," Wanda and Julie cried together.

JANUARY

It is good to finally turn the corner, leaving the holidays behind, and see the clean sweep of the year lying before us. January can be many things, cold, icy, warm, clear, dark, hopeful. But above all, his icy expanse must be crossed, despite the conditions and obstacles we will encounter along the way.

From Mrs. Lilac's Journal

January brought the coldest temperatures Mrs Lilac could remember. One day of frigid cold followed another, with the wind sweeping over the meadow like a freight train. The furnace moaned and groaned but kept on running, and Scrappy and Stormy refused to venture far from the front porch. Many of her clients chose not to brave the cold, and the phone was silent.

Mrs. Lilac felt at times that her heart was as cold as the outside temperatures. No matter what she chose to do to keep the house and her life cozy and warm, the cold crept in through the walls of the cottage and her heart.

One morning, when the temperature was five below zero, she stood at the sitting room window and stared off across the winter emptiness. The meadow was devoid of life. The trees looked as sad and lonely as she felt inside. Only a few strips of snow remained. The farms were quite visible in the distance, and the sun was bright but seemed to offer little warmth. The stream was so icy, mists rose from it at various places, but because it rose as a spring far in the distant hills, and ran so quickly past the cottage, it very seldom froze over. She thought of the months stretching ahead, months that would bring major changes to her life, but ones that had to be faced, nonetheless. She could ignore everything, and not even think of preparing for the move that seemed inevitable, or she could start thinking of what she would take and what she would leave behind. The worst thing that could happen was that she would just do nothing, and then have Mr. Gately take legal action and have her removed. She shook herself back from that thought. She knew she would soon have to start making plans and decisions.

She turned from the window and went into the living room with her mug of coffee. She sat down at the table as she often did and picked up her cards. Mrs. Lilac didn't believe in reading too often for herself. But since it was the first part of the year, perhaps it wouldn't hurt to see if she could get anything of substance or guidance from them. When she had first started her readings years before, the cards had been kind to her, and she was able to get quite a lot of help and guidance for herself. But, as the years had passed, the information seemed less and less where she was concerned. Sometimes, when she asked a particular question, the cards were only paper and there was no subconscious magic to be felt or seen.

This morning, she laid out a spread of cards that seemed to show a bright and hopeful future for her. They seemed to say that things would work out, that solutions would be found to her current dilemma. What she didn't like was that several negative cards appeared in prominent positions. The Tower stood in a future position, but so did The World and a card that represented great happiness. It seemed to her that there was a puzzle to be solved before the answers would come. It looked as though an unexpected event would hold the revelation she needed for her future. She certainly hoped that some of what the cards showed would happen, but knowing her recent luck, she wasn't so sure.

Her personal reading was interrupted by the ringing phone, and Mrs. Lilac came back to herself in a rush. Suddenly it was just a normal morning and there were clients to come and the regular chores of the day to be done.

The call was from Rose Wilder. She had last read for her and her daughter, Serena, in the fall. Rose seemed very excited on the phone.

"I've got to see you, Mrs. Lilac," she said. "Serena, too. Things have happened, and we need to talk to you as soon as possible."

Mrs. Lilac was frankly glad to hear from her, since there had been few calls in the past days.

"Well, I could actually see you this evening," Mrs. Lilac told her. "The cold has kept people away, and things are very slow here. Are you sure you won't mind coming out with the temperature so low?"

"Oh, heavens no, Mrs. Lilac. We're used to the cold. I'm originally from Canada, you know. We knew all about the cold there."

They set a time for six that evening, and Mrs. Lilac went on with her chores.

The phone rang again, mid-afternoon. It was Annabelle Wilkins.

Mrs. Lilac was surprised to hear from her. She hadn't seen her friend since the early fall when she'd come out to collect her roots and herbs along the stream, and they'd had lunch together.

"How are you, honey," Annabelle's voice boomed. "I have been thinking about you a lot lately. But I've had a lot of trouble here. My sister took a bad turn just before Christmas, but I got her back. Yes, right now, I got her back. And this terrible mean cold don't do too well for my arthritis. Some days I want to go right back to Mississippi, I do. I just want to get on a bus and go right back home. But as long as I'm needed here, I'll stay."

"It's good to hear from you, dear," Mrs. Lilac said. "I sent you a card at Christmas. But I'm not sure I got the right address on it."

"Oh, yes you did, honey. I got the card. I just didn't send any myself. It was all I could do to fix dinner for all the fools who showed up here for a taste of my southern cooking!" Annabelle laughed loudly. "Now honey," she went on, "about that other business we talked about when I was out there that day, and we had such a nice lunch together and you told me about that snake of a landlord, and how he's making you move. Well, I just made it my business to stop there on my way home that day. Practically forced myself into his office where he was sitting, all high and mighty. Told him I had a nephew who was looking for work, and while he was getting me the application, I just picked up a couple little personal things from his desk. So, honey, just like I promised, I'm working for you. And like that old saying, what goes around comes around. And girlie, don't you worry, old Annabelle's working her magic, deed I am, and as soon as the weather clears, I'll be out to see you. We'll have a good laugh. It'll do us both good.. Now you take care, hear?"

And just as quickly as the call had come, Annabelle's voice was gone. Mrs. Lilac shook her head. She did not personally believe that Annabelle had the kind of powers she claimed, but she shivered a little at the thought of her stopping at Mr. Gately's office that day. But she knew better than to challenge another persons beliefs. It was best sometimes to just keep silent and go along with the game. What in the world would Annabel come up with next?

At promptly six that evening, Rose Wilder and Serena appeared at the door. By this time, it was dark and colder than it had been that morning, but the wind was still and that was a relief. Mrs Lilac was very glad to see another human face, and she ushered them in and took their coats.

They were both so cold they didn't seem able to speak at first but once they had adjusted to the warmer air, Rose became quite animated. Serena could barely contain herself.

Finally, Serena held out her hand, and Mrs. Lilac was shocked to see an engagement ring on her finger. "Look Mrs. Lilac, I'm getting married," Serena cried. "Bernie and I got back together, and he proposed to me on Christmas day. We want to get married in June."

"Do you think that's too soon, Mrs. Lilac?" Rose asked, shaking her head, when Mrs. Lilac had given Serena a warm hug, and they were all seated at the table. "I mean, don't you think they should wait another year, perhaps? So that they have time to get to know each other and to find out if this is really what they want."

"Oh mother, why must you always go on so," Serena asked "You know I have my mind made up, and Bernie and I are going to move to Washington right after the wedding. You see, Mrs. Lilac, I graduate in May, and Senator Hackman has offered me a job in his office there. Daddy has known him for years, and he's aware of my passion for politics. It's a start for me, and Bernie wants to come, too. I just can't see us going there together unless we get married before we go."

So Shirl was just a diversion?" Mrs. Lilac asked.

"Oh, just like you said, Bernie was trying to make me jealous. He called me, right after I saw you that day, and we got together and had a long talk. I told him what I liked and didn't like about his nature. I told him I couldn't stand him always being in control. It turns out we just can't be away from each other for long, Mrs. Lilac. I love him more than I knew."

"We can't stand in the way of our hearts sometimes, dear," Mrs. Lilac told her quietly. "It seems there are times they know best. Often, when we least expect it, something happens in the area of love that is almost miraculous. I think you already know what you are going to do, but if you think you'd like the advice of the cards, I'd very much like to lay them out for you."

Rose had sat silent while her daughter had done the talking. But now, she started up again with a rather negative attitude. "I just don't know Mrs. Lilac, as a mother, I just seem to have reservations about this. There's so much to think of, Serena's health and all. And how do we know they'll even like it in Washington?"

"Oh mother, your problem is you just don't want to let your little girl go. You know that's it, why don't you admit it?" Serena's face took on a kind of angry look and she pushed her dark hair out of her eyes.

Rose was silent as Mrs. Lilac offered Serena the cards to shuffle. When she was finished, Mrs. Lilac took them and started putting them down on the table.

"Your cards show a new beginning for you, Serena, a fresh start," she said. "And while the path you are taking is not always going to be easy, it seems, even at your young age, you have the wisdom and fortitude to make this work. I do see the marriage, so I can assure you, Rose, it's going to happen in spite of your doubts, though well founded, they might be. So I would suggest you go with this rather than oppose it, otherwise I think you might end up with some health problems of your own."

"Do you think we can get this whole thing together by then?" Rose asked. "The kids want to be married in the Caronsburg Star Theater. That's where they met, Mrs. Lilac, as you predicted, when they were in the Drama Guild play. Do you think we can do all this in the little time we have?"

Mrs. Lilac lay down another spread of cards. "The wedding will go beautifully," she said. "There is happiness and good will all around. I see nothing that wants to stand in the way. And the weather will cooperate as well. And also, you will have a happy life together in Washington. Just remember that nothing in this life is perfect. So what if the ceremony may have a few glitches? And what if you and Bernie have a misunderstanding now and again? We grow from our mistakes and our differences. Serena, I'd be a fool if I tried to tell you to do other than what you already know in your heart. I approve of your plan, and I wish you happiness and joy."

"Oh, thank you Mrs. Lilac, you are such a dear. And I want you to take part in our wedding. You told me long ago that I would meet my true love and that we would someday be married. Everything you predicted for me has come true. You will never know how much your help and kindness has meant to me."

"We want to have the wedding reception out at the Mountainside Inn," Rose said. "Oh my, there's just so much to prepare for."

"But prepare you will," Mrs. Lilac told her. "Whatever you do, please try to enjoy everything about it. It's a once in a life time experience."

"Perhaps you could write a poem for the ceremony," Serena said suddenly. "That would be lovely, having you read it there that day. Mother says you write beautifully."

Mrs. Lilac was taken aback. Write a poem for a wedding? Where would she find the inspiration? Where could she possibly start?

"Oh, I don't know about that," Mrs Lilac sputtered. "That's a big request, and I don't know if I could do it."

"Just promise me you'll try," Serena said. "You don't have to say yes or no just now. Take some time to think about it, okay?"

Mrs. Lilac promised her she would, and after the two of them had left her, she stood still in the middle of the room for a long moment. Her mind whirled with the thought of the wonderful things that had happened to Serena, after all she had suffered. The universe could be fair and kind, after all. But could she see herself standing in front of a large group of people at a wedding reading a poem? She certainly was not sure of that.

A few days later Mrs. Lilac looked out her bedroom window and was surprised by the changes she saw. The temperature had risen, and there was a mist rising from the meadow. In the early morning sunlight it took on a pink glow. Was this the January thaw? Mrs. Lilac quickly sat at her desk and wrote down a few lines of poetry that suddenly came to her.

Pink meadow morning
over sheets of snow,
Tell me, oh tell me,
where did summer go?

Now in darkest winter
This sudden teasing thaw,
and summer taunting and flaunting
tries to fool us all.

For the first time in days, she took Scrappy on his leash down to the stream. Her coat was warm, and the air, though still chilly, was bearable. The walk down to the water was worth it. The scents coming across the meadow were clean and fresh. Even Stormy had come down with them, raising his paws delicately with each step. Both of the pets stood momentarily, as she did, sniffing the air as though they were smelling future days, days when they would come here in better weather and really enjoy the incredible sights and sounds of summer that they remembered.

But then, she realized, there would be no summer days here again, and later, back at the house, this came to her quite suddenly again when the phone rang. It was Fern and she seemed quite cheery.

"My Dear, I have some good news for you," she said excitedly, " I think I have found you a new home! It's a first floor apartment in a house just up the street from me. It has a small yard and garden, and an entrance at the back. I think there are five rooms in all, and it will become available June 1ˢᵗ. It would be perfect for you. They even allow pets."

Mrs Lilac was silent. It seemed there was nothing for her to say. After her walk down to the stream, her heart wasn't into thinking of living in an apartment in town. But she must not let Fern think she was unappreciative.

"Thank you, Fern, for looking out for me," she said, half heartedly. "Have you seen the place? I mean, have you gone through the rooms and all?"

"Well no, dear, because there is a family living there now. They're moving into a home of their own in the Spring. I think they will be going in April. I know the lady who owns the place, Mrs. Kendall. I ran into her at the Grill one morning, and since I knew she had several apartment houses, I told her about you and when you would be needing a place. She told me about the apartment, and also said she will hold it for you until you have a chance to look at it. She said she'd let me know as soon as the family moved out."

Fern was soon off on a story about a man she had gone to school with who had just discovered he had cancer. His wife was already very ill with a heart condition. Fern had a habit of changing boats in mid- stream, and Mrs. Lilac only half listened until she was able to get off the phone by telling her friend there was a client at the door.

She certainly was glad Fern was keeping an eye out for her, and at least the apartment was a place she could possibly go to for a while until she got her bearings. She supposed that having a roof over her head was the most important thing. But there was so much to think of. And what about her readings? How could she possibly get away with them right in the middle of town? What if her neighbors opposed her? These were issues she would have to take up when the time came.

The shift in the weather brought several calls for appointments that morning. The rising temperatures seemed to have brought folks out from their warm dens, and Mrs. Lilac was glad. One of the calls she received was from Mrs. Simmons, a lady she had read for in July. She seemed quite excited on the phone, and Mrs. Lilac only vaguely remembered her.

Seeing her at the door the next afternoon, helped Mrs. Lilac recall some of what they had talked about the previous summer. Her mother's death, an alcoholic husband.

Mrs. Simmons had a new hair do, and was wearing a gray business suit under her coat. She had a bright smile on her face, and when they were seated at the table, she began to speak excitedly.

"I took your advice, Mrs. Lilac." She said. "I found a job! It's only part time, but I love it. I'm working in the high school in the afternoons, in the business office. It's wonderful, it gets me away from the house. And the most important thing is, I'm seeing a counselor, just as you suggested. It's made all the difference for me."

"I'm so happy for you," Mrs Lilac told her. "I remember you were quite upset when I talked to you that day."

"Yes I was, Mrs. Lilac, and something you told me then has kept me going. You said, "work at strengthening you, your husband is beyond your help." Remember?"

"I can't always recall what I say in the readings, but sometimes I do. I remember you told me about your husband, his drinking, and his abusive habits. How is he taking this new image?"

"He doesn't like any of it, Mrs. Lilac." Mrs. Simmons said. "He's fought me every step of the way. But I took charge of my own life. I don't know where I'm going to end up, but I'm heading in the right direction."

"And is he still drinking?"

"He says he's cut back, but I know better. He drinks every night. He's sneaky with not keeping his booze in the house. But we have an old refrigerator in the garage, and he goes back and forth to that, night after night. After I was here that first time, I told him everything you said. I know I shouldn't have, but I wanted to shock him back to reality. You mentioned how, if he didn't stop his habit, it would kill him. I told him that and everything else. I just wanted to get him to see what he was doing to himself. I told him I was coming here again today, and you know what Mrs. Lilac, he says he's going to come to see you himself."

"Well, let him come if he wants," Mrs. Lilac said soberly, "but the message he gets from me will be the same one. I have no sympathy for alcoholism. None whatsoever. Only the individual has the power to change and to heal."

When they finally got to the cards, Mrs. Lilac lay them out quietly in the usual pattern.

"I'm really amazed," she told her client. "You have made some wonderful progress, and your life does seem to be going in a new direction. I see you going back to school, perhaps, continuing to learn new lessons. At some time, I see you finding a more suitable career for yourself, working at something you enjoy, something you may always have thought of doing. You still look back with sadness at the loss of your mother, and at the thought that your children no longer need you as they once did. But I also see grandchildren down the road, and time spent with them may heal many wounds."

Mrs. Lilac stopped a moment and pondered the cards. There was still darkness there, sadness, sorrow, and perhaps at some time her client would be on her own. Her husband was surrounded by guilt and fear. She somehow felt he was on a tragic course and that there was no hope for him if he didn't immediately get some help for his addiction. "Have you thought of divorcing your husband?" Mrs. Lilac asked. "So many of the future cards show a separation, a possible end to your relationship? And he looks even worse in the cards I'm seeing here today. I am very fearful of where he will end up if he doesn't change the course he seems to be on."

"Yes, I have thought of divorce, Mrs Lilac." Mrs. Simmons lowered her head. "Right now I can't do it, for financial reasons. But I have a good friend who is in real estate. She wants me to get my real estate license and join her firm. It's something I've thought of doing for a long time, and when you mentioned going to school, it is something I'm seriously thinking of doing. I realize, going into the business is risky. So many people think it's an easy way to make a living. I know how hard it will be, yet I'm up to the challenge. Now that I'm finding myself again, I'm willing to give it a try. And when I do begin to make a decent living, you can be sure that I will definitely be divorcing my husband. He knows full well what I'm planning. Perhaps that is why the cards look so bad. I'm frightened to think of what his life may become once I am gone."

"I understand," Mrs. Lilac said. "But as you've already mentioned, it is good that you've finally put yourself first. You have something to look forward to now. And the happiness to come will be richly deserved."

"Thank you Mrs. Lilac. But you must know you've helped me more than you realize. If I hadn't come that first time for a reading, I think I'd still be back there, frightened and unhappy. You've helped give me the desire to change."

"That's very kind of you," Mrs. Lilac told her. "It always makes me feel good to know that something I've said or done has given someone the incentive for a better life."

The January thaw was brief, and one day the TV in the bedroom began warning of an approaching storm that could reach blizzard proportions in her area. Mrs. Lilac took note, and decided she'd better get out to the store and buy some supplies, in case she got snowed in. The parking lot at the local Food Mart was jammed, but she found a parking spot and got into the store without a problem. She loaded the necessary items into her cart, and was getting ready to go through the checkout, when she spotted Mr. Gately ahead of her. He was pushing a cart, next to a woman with a cane. She was walking slowly, and gave the impression of illness. Mrs. Lilac didn't feel as though she wanted to run into them, so she held back, and went into another aisle where she could be an observer. She knew Mr. Gately was married, but she had only seen his wife once, several years ago, when she paid the rent. Mr. Gately obviously cared about her very much, by the way he hovered near her and held onto her arm while pushing the cart at the same time. Mrs. Lilac wondered what might be wrong with her. She seemed quite tired and her face was ashen.

Mrs. Lilac was only home from the store a short time when it began to snow. It came down very lightly at first, but as the afternoon wore along, it grew heavier. She watched it from the bedroom window. Before she knew it, the creek bank and the meadow were covered in white, and it was piling up fast. By the time it was dark, the wind had kicked up, and she realized they were in for a wintry siege.

All through the night, the wind roared. She tried to sleep, but just dozed off from time to time, only to be awakened by a particularly loud burst of wind. Her biggest fear was that the electricity would go off, and that the furnace would stop working. But the small lamp in the corner stayed lit and the furnace continued to run, though it creaked and groaned. When she couldn't sleep, Mrs. Lilac thought about many things. Her mind spun with all that had occurred over the past few months, and even more at the thought of what lay ahead. And so, to calm herself during the storm, she tried to think of pleasant things. Of course, she found herself thinking of Bill Green. She had not heard from him since Christmas, but she went over their dinner together. Her thoughts lingered long over the goodbyes under the stars that night.

Morning finally came. By daylight, the wind had died down a bit, but when she looked out the window, she was stunned by how much snow had fallen. Judging by her eye's first glance, it was at least two feet. The wind was drifting it everywhere, across the meadow and the yard. When she managed to open the front door, she saw that her car was completely drifted over in the driveway, and there was only a narrow strip of open area where she could let Scrappy take care of his morning business. Scrappy loved the snow, but this was far above his head, and there would be no frolicking in it for him today. Mrs. Lilac was used to the winters in this place. She had learned not to get too alarmed at such seasonal developments, but as she grew older, she found it was harder to sit by and feel so helpless. How long would it be before things were normal again, and she had some clients who might help pass the lonely winter hours?

The snow plow finally rumbled along the road in the late afternoon. Before that, she had not been able to see any sign of macadam. All the boundaries of her world had been lost. Now you could at least see where the road was, and it was comforting to know it was there, almost like the future, winding away into a pure white world.

It was sometime after dark, and she was sitting down at the table with a steaming cup of tea, when she heard the loud sound of machinery outside the cottage. At the door, she was surprised to find Bill Green and David Tarner. They were both bundled up like Eskimos in all the winter clothing they could possibly put on. They were grinning widely, though their cheeks were red from the wind and cold. A huge tractor sat, still running, in the driveway.

"We thought we'd come and shovel you out, and see that you were alright," David said, excitedly.

"I didn't like the idea of your being out here all alone during the storm," Bill Green said, quite seriously. "You know my phone number, and I want you to call me when you need something."

"Now you have two guardian angels, " David said, laughing. She noticed how he glanced at her from the corner of his eye. His sense of humor was endearing at times.

Mrs. Lilac insisted they come in and have a hot drink before they did any plowing or shoveling, and it made her feel good to offer them each coffee or tea and a huge slice of lemon pound cake. They both enjoyed it immensely.

"You shouldn't have taken the time to worry over me, Mrs. Lilac said, when they'd finished their cake and were sipping large mugs of coffee. I'm used to this kind of weather, and I did manage to get in a few extra supplies yesterday."

"Still, I want you to know, I'm there if you need me," Bill said.

"Yes, and if next year I can't come because of school, I'm turning you over to him," David said, still grinning.

"Well, there probably isn't going to be a next year," Mrs. Lilac said then, sadly.

"What do you mean, Mrs. Barnes?" David asked.

"Well I'm going to have to move, David. Mr. Gately gave me the news last summer. I just haven't told you. I didn't want anyone to worry over me. I have to be out by the end of May."

But where will you go," Bill Green asked, his face suddenly quite serious. "You're not going far away, I hope?"

"I want to stay here in the area," she told them. "My friend Fern is looking in town for me, and there is a possible place, though I haven't seen it yet."

"You've been here a long time, haven't you Mrs. Barnes?" David asked.

"Nearly twenty years, David," she told him. It's been the only real home I've ever had."

They were all silent then, and when the two of them got up to go out and tackle the snow, Bill Green patted her on the back. "Don't worry Betty," He said. "Something will come up for you. Sometimes I think I'm a little psychic myself, but somehow I don't see you having to move from here."

That was all he said, and she stood at the window and watched as they plowed the driveway and then took shovels and a broom and removed the snow from the car, porch and walk.

When they were finished, they came to the door and she asked them in again. They declined, and David said, "We have to be going, Mrs. Barnes, we have a few more folks to help yet tonight."

As they were leaving, Mrs. Lilac hugged them both, despite their heavy, cold clothing.

"Remember what I told you," Bill Green said, as they left. "I mean it."

And then they were gone, and she stood at the window wondering what he wanted her to remember. Did he mean about calling if she needed anything, or that bit about his being psychic and not seeing her having to move?

Bill Green psychic? She pondered that. It wouldn't surprise her. He seemed to know how little it took to endear himself to her. He seemed to understand the longing in a lonely woman's heart. If only his psychic moment was real and there would be a next year and a next year after that in this place. She realized that home is in the heart, but she found nothing at all wrong with the four walls and roof of this particular cottage. Why couldn't Mr. Gately be more human? He seemed to have some feelings, by the way he had hovered over his wife at the store that day. But what was she, Mrs. Lilac, to him? Only a strange woman who delved into realms he would never understand.

FEBRUARY

I have always felt that February is less harsh and unreasonable than his predecessor, and a bit of a romantic as well. Perhaps both their hearts are made of ice, having come from the same wintry kingdom, but February's heart can often be a warm and tender place.

From Mrs. Lilac's Journal.

Slowly at first, but then at a quickened pace as the temperature rose, the snow began to melt. Mrs. Lilac looked out at the creek bank on an early February morning and felt a kind of renewal seep into her spirit. The sun shone brightly, and the meadow expanse was radiant with light. Already, long strips of earth began appearing from place to place. The sound of melting snow, dripping down from the roof above, was like music to her. She began imagining spring.

The pets had both been sticking close to the house since the big snow. The boundaries of their world was the driveway and the far fence. There had been no walks in the junk yard or along the stream or road. But Mrs. Lilac could tell they would be able to reclaim the creek bank in just a few days.

There had been calls every day for readings, though things were still a bit slow there, as most of her former clients seemed to be hibernating. Her first client that afternoon was a gentleman whose voice she hadn't recognized, but by the sound of things, he had a problem he was trying to sort out. Usually with her male clients, their problems seemed mostly to deal with a relationship gone sour.

Mrs. Lilac thought it best to not think too deeply about her own problems just now and to concentrate on those of others. She usually always had some insight there, but when it came to her own, she often just worried until her mind shut down. She had made up her mind to follow the path Fern had laid out for her for now. At least she had some vague notion of where she would end up, even if the whole thing seemed to be happening against her will.

She took Scrappy out on his leash. Stormy stayed behind in the window. Only a light coat was necessary. The temperature seemed nearly balmy after the last few weeks, and the air was pure. The scents, of the earth and melting snow, were exquisite. She breathed deeply as she stood there waiting for Scruffy to be done with his morning ritual. Looking down at him as he dug his way into a pile of snow, a spectacle in two shades of white, she realized that she was more concerned about her pets than she was of herself. She could sleep anywhere, even in a tent in a field. But it would be the saddest thing to uproot her pets and take them to a world that was strange and unfamiliar. A small yard in the center of town was nothing compared to what they already had here.

The phone was ringing when she made her way back into the house. It was Fern.

"I"m having a little party here on the Friday evening after Valentine's Day." Fern said quickly, without the usual first greeting. She seemed a bit excited, so Mrs. Lilac figured this was a spur of the moment thing. "I wonder if you could come and do some romantic readings for the girls. I'm going to have about a dozen guests. Just a little fluff and color for the season, that's all, not a big fuss. But I want you to come dressed for the part. Wear something red, and please, lots of jewelry. The girls will get a kick out of it."

"Well, I'm sure I can come." Mrs. Lilac answered. "I usually don't have clients on a Friday, anyway."

"Good," Fern said, and hung up without another word. Mrs. Lilac stood there and shook her head, still holding the phone in her hand. She wondered how, as flighty as she was, that Fern could coordinate anything as serious as a move for her. She would have to ask some serious questions of her friend before she could rest a bit easier. Also, she would have to press the issue of when she would be able to look at the place. How could she be sure it was not totally negative in some way?

Her first client of the afternoon was indeed unfamiliar to her. When she opened the door the first thing she noticed was the pale, sickly look on his face. He was a man in his fifties, she guessed, tall and thin, with graying hair. She held out her hand to shake his and noticed, that as he extended it to her, it was shaking. He was dressed in a blue flannel shirt and gray slacks.

Mrs. Lilac felt ill at ease. There was something about this man she didn't like, but she wasn't quite sure what it was. She wished for once she had dressed in one of her character outfits. Instead, she had on a simple white blouse and blue sweater over a dark pair of slacks. She felt as though she had nothing to hide behind.

When they were finally seated at the table, the man stared at her with a dark serious look on his face.

"How could you say all those terrible things about me?" he asked.

Mrs. Lilac was taken aback. "I'm sure I don't know what you mean," Mrs. Lilac blurted out.

"Don't you know who I am?"

"I've never seen you before in my life," Mrs. Lilac told him.

"I'm Glenn Simmons." The man said sharply. "You've read for my wife. And, thanks to you, she's acting like a nut and threatening to leave me."

June Simmons! Mrs. Lilac remembered. It all came back to her in a rush. The alcoholic husband, the control and verbal abuse. Now here he was sitting right in front of her, and he seemed not to be very pleased with her. She tried to remain calm and waited for him to speak.

"You, certainly made me out to be a fool!" Mr. Simmons went on. "So I drink a little, what's that to you? It's none of your business to be talking to my wife like that about me. Especially telling her to leave me. You made me sound like a monster. It's made me sick!"

Anger rose in Mrs. Lilac. She always tried to be a nice person, but she could defend herself if stirred.

"Just a minute Mr. Simmons! Keep one thing in mind. Your wife came to me, not the other way around. She was a very unhappy woman when she came. I gave her a little advice, helped her see her true potential. She's trying to find herself again. She's working at making plans for her future. What was wrong about that?" She went on without giving him a chance to speak. "As for you, I said nothing to your wife that wasn't true. You are an alcoholic, and it will kill you in the end unless you choose to stop what you're doing. Is that shedding any negativity on you? No, it's simply shedding light on the destructive habit you have, one that I'm too familiar with. My ex-husband was an alcoholic. I choose to leave him, because I knew there was nothing I could do to help him. And I wanted a life without the abuse and hell of it. Your wife seems to be making the same choice for herself. You, at least, still have the time to try to change the course of what is happening. Why don't you think of doing that without blaming me for your woes!"

Mrs. Lilac was silent for a moment. She noticed her breath was coming fast. Mr. Simmons had really stirred her up. Now he sat opposite her, eyes down. He seemed to be thinking.

"But it's as though you predicted my death," he said finally, in a calmer tone. "That's the thing I find hard to take. Do you know what that's done to me?"

"I never predict death," Mrs. Lilac broke in. "In your case, I have had enough experience with alcoholism to know that the disease kills. I had two women in the past year who lost husbands to it. And I'm sure they were just as insistent as you are that they had no real problem, except that they drank a little. I personally think alcoholism is a dirty, selfish habit. It destroys lives. And Mr. Simmons, unless you choose to stop, it will destroy yours."

Mrs. Lilac was surprised to see Mr. Simmons suddenly wracked by sobs. She was a bit stunned and quickly thought to offer him a tissue, though there were no tears in sight. But his hands shook, and his general appearance told her he was deeply distressed.

Surely she couldn't have stunned him that much by what she'd said. Was it his wife's preparing to leave him, was it something deeper?

He finally regained his composure, and Mrs. Lilac sat staring at his face. He had the look of alcoholism about him, in the color of his skin, in the twist of his mouth. There was that look of sadness there also, a need for pity, but beyond that was a deeper layer. Yes, she could tell by looking into his eyes that there was something more that was troubling him. Was it her intuition, a flash of her psychic ability, or just the pained fearful look in his eye that told her Mr. Simmons had a deeper secret? And there was a sharper bit, something she recognized but didn't. Was it the tendency to abuse that his wife had told her of, or was it something darker, almost criminal, that lurked in his character? Mrs. Lilac felt a self protective instinct rise in her. Whatever she said to him from here on needed to be thought through, carefully measured.

"I'm assuming you would like cards read for you," Mrs. Lilac said, in an even voice. "Perhaps I can give you a little help or insight into what you might do to change the situation you find yourself in."

Mr. Simmons was silent for a moment, his eyes darting back and forth. Then he nodded his head. His hands were still shaking when Mrs. Lilac handed him the deck of cards. He took them as though they would burn his hands and the shuffling process was quick.

Mrs. Lilac took the cards back from him and began laying them down. She saw at once his drinking problem, and the situation with his wife. It looked as though she had indeed made up her mind to leave him when she became more self sufficient. She also saw that Mr. Simmons might very well give up his habit at some future time. Dark cards in future positions indicated prison, a hospital, or both. This wasn't going to be easy to talk to the man about. But it was in the past that Mrs. Lilac began to pick up something dark and secretive. It was partly from the cards, partly from her subconscious voice. Something sudden and unexpected had happened to Mr. Simmons. There was a dark night, an accident, a young girl, incredible anxiety. She suddenly remembered the same sort of thing in his wife's cards the previous summer. Mrs. Simmons hadn't known who the cards were indicating. And then a thought hit Mrs. Lilac, like a brick striking her in the brain. Was Glenn Simmons the hit and run driver who killed Becky Wilson?

Mrs. Lilac's heart was beating out of control. She must be careful not to show any kind of emotion. She finished laying out the last few cards and began speaking in what she hoped was a calm, easy voice. She glanced up from the cards and saw that Mr. Simmons was watching her, his face taut and serious. He seemed to be checking for any sign that she had seen anything that might unearth his secret, but she gave no indication that she saw anything dark.

"I'm glad to see that there is a chance for you to turn things around in your life," Mrs. Lilac began. "I do see you getting help for your addiction at some time in the future, perhaps in time to save your marriage. I also see health problems, but if you make an effort, I think you can reach some kind of balance there."

Mrs. Lilac stopped and stared at Mr Simmons for a few seconds. He seemed a bit calmer and his breath came easier. His eyes were still wary and watchful.

"I know you feel anger toward me for talking to your wife as I did. But I would do it again if I had it to do over. You need to take a good look at how your alcoholism effects others. If quitting the habit seems impossible for you, perhaps you should seek help."

There was more after that, but whatever was said seemed a blur to Mrs. Lilac. She remembered Glenn Simmons shaking her hand with his own very icy palm and then going out the door. At least his anger seemed vented and there was a calmer look on his face. The fear still lay there, however, at the bottom of his eyes.

Mrs. Lilac sat alone on the sofa for a long time after Glenn Simmons left. Outside, darkness had fallen, and she had lost track of time.

Was Glenn Simmons the hit and run driver? At the moment of laying down the cards she was nearly certain, the vision she had was too real to be imagination. But now she wasn't so sure. There were a lot of tragedies in the world, perhaps the cards were indicating something no one could even remember. Perhaps a dead relative, gone long before even he could recall. She went back in her mind to his wife's reading in the summer. She had given no indication that she knew anything that had happened to a young girl as Mrs. Lilac had described.

And what if Glenn Simmons was the guilty party? What could she do with the information? Take it to the police and have them laugh her out of the station? No, she could only sit still with her suspicions and trust the universe to work the whole thing out.

Mrs. Lilac went back to the table and shuffled the cards again and lay down a spread. Yes, Glenn Simmons was keeping a secret, they told her, something he didn't want anyone to know. It was eating away at him, driving him nearly insane. What she had told his wife was only secondary to the real reason for his visit today. Glenn Simmons wanted to see how much she knew. For, like a lot of people, he must have believed that she could look at a persons face and pick up every detail of their history. She could only hope that she had masked well enough what she had really seen in his cards.

But where had his suspicions come from? Mrs. Simmons said she had told him everything they had discussed during that first reading. Obviously she must have mentioned the facts of the accident and the dead girl. Could Glenn Simmons have been the caller who had plagued her during the Fall? Once, the stranger had asked her if she knew who he was.

Oh, it was almost too much to contemplate. She had to leave it alone for awhile and let her thoughts come back into place. Perhaps tomorrow or the next day she could think of the whole thing with a little more clarity. Perhaps then she would know what to do with her suspicions.

Until then, it seemed to her, she was in a position of safety.

The next day, her readings went much easier, and she tried to put thoughts of Glenn Simmons behind her. Things became more upbeat, especially when one of her previous clients showed up in the afternoon with a surprise for her. The visitor was Richard Coleman, a man she had read for many times during the previous year. Dick was a likeable fellow, but at times he could be a rather difficult client, because he had tested Mrs. Lilac during every reading. His wife had decided to end their marriage, and he had spent a hard year hoping that they could be reunited. Mrs. Lilac had been there during every difficult step of the way.

She was surprised to find him at her door that afternoon with a large Valentine Heart filled with candy. Dick was quite a handsome chap, a bit overweight, with thinning blond hair and blue eyes. He had a winning smile and a natural sense of humor.

"This is for you Mrs. Lilac." he told her. "This is for putting up with me, and for helping me get through my difficult time. I want you to know you are more than a card reader to me. I feel you are a friend."

"Oh Dick," Mrs. Lilac said. "How kind of you. I needed a little lift today."

She asked him to sit and offered him coffee, and when they were comfortable, Mrs Lilac asked him how things were going. He'd called her back in the summer and given her the good news that he and his wife had gotten back together.

"Well," he told her, "We reunited again in June and renewed our vows. You told me we would be together again in June, and it was June the twenty eighth when I moved back in. Things are going well. I think we both needed the time apart, and she came to the realization that she still loved me after all."

"I'm so happy for you , Dick." Mrs. Lilac told him. " It makes me feel so good to know you are happy again. You were one of my special cases. And heaven knows you worked me hard enough!"

They both laughed.   Dick went on with his story and Mrs. Lilac remembered that his wife had resented the fact that he had bought an antique car without her knowledge, and that was the event that triggered her desire to end the marriage. "I came to realize that it wasn't just the car, it was a lot of other things that caused our crisis." Dick told her. "We had been growing apart for a long time, and neither of us realized it. It seems to me that our separation helped us both understand that.   He stopped for a moment and took a sip of his coffee.

"But you know what, Mrs. Lilac? It was the help you gave me, the little bits of knowledge, the suggestions, that have helped me become a better husband. I'll never forget you for that."

Mrs. Lilac was speechless as Dick went on with his praise.   But since praise was something she was never able to take well, she shut it out a bit and found herself suddenly thinking of Bill Green. It was almost as though it was he sitting there with her and not Dick. It was his face she saw, and his words she was listening to. It was wonderful of Dick to have brought her the candy, but she wished it had been Bill. Dick had become like a son to her, and she liked him very much. She suddenly realized that both he and Bill Green had the same gentle kind of spirit, that underneath the rough exterior there was sensitivity and compassion. She hadn't seen Bill since the night he had come to plow her snow, and she suddenly realized she had missed him.

Perhaps it's just because it's closing in on Valentines Day, Mrs. Lilac thought, when she had hugged Dick and he was gone. She suddenly decided it would be nice to bake Bill a coconut cake and take it to him before the fourteenth. It wasn't like she would be giving him a gift for the holiday. It was just being nice. And she owed him something for his kindness in shoveling her snow.   So when she was finished for the night, she found herself mixing and baking. It helped her to keep her mind off the more serious issues of her life, the impending move, Glenn Simmons.

She delivered the cake to Bill the next day. She felt a bit awkward, but he didn't seem surprised to see her there at his door. He even asked her in while he took the cake to the kitchen.

While he was gone Mrs. Lilac took a look around the living room. It was nicely decorated in a country style, and Mrs. Lilac had the feeling that nothing had been changed since his wife's death. The family photos were evident and it was a woman's hand that had chosen the color scheme, the fabric and paint.

"Thank you for the cake, Betty," Bill said, coming back into the room.

"I wanted to do something to thank you for the snow shoveling you did for me," she told him,

feeling suddenly that she was an intruder here in this place where his wife's presence seemed everywhere.

"You didn't need to do that," he told her. Then he looked down at the floor for a moment before going on, "I was wondering if you might go out to dinner with me some evening before the end of the month. I'd like to pay you back for the fine meal you gave me at Christmas."

"I'd like that very much," Mrs. Lilac said, her mood cheering a bit.

"There's an old Inn in Fairview, a few miles from here, close to the state line." he said. "I'll set up the reservations. Will the 24th work for you? It's a Saturday."

"My book is always open on weekends," she told him.

"Good, then I'll pick you up around five," he said.

A date with Bill Green! Her heart was beating wildly all the way home. She hadn't expected that at all, but now she had something to look forward to. She was acting like a teenager, she knew, but she couldn't help herself. Already she was thinking ahead. What would she wear? What in the world would they have to talk about? Surely they'd said everything there was to say at Christmas. But suddenly she realized it didn't matter as long as it was his face she was staring at across the table.

The evening of Fern's party came more quickly than Mrs. Lilac realized. She spent some time nervously getting herself together. She put on a red dress as Fern had suggested and wore a red scarf around her neck. As for the jewelry, she wore only two rings, both large faux rubies, one on either hand. She also wore a couple of colorful red combs in her hair. A fancy white lace shawl completed the outfit.

Fern's house was decorated gaily for the affair. There was crepe paper and lace everywhere, and a beautiful bouquet of roses in the center of the table. Fern herself was in a happy kind of mood. She had laid out quite a spread of food, a large meat platter, another vegetable tray with dip, a variety of cheeses and crackers, and a beautiful cake decorated in pink and white icing.

Fern had painted a small oil about six inches square. It was of two red roses next to a a small crystal heart. She had each guest who came in put their name on a piece of paper and she informed them all that the painting would be given to the person whose name was drawn at the end of the party. Mrs. Lilac made sure hers was put in with the rest for she was a great admirer of Fern's work. The guests were all ladies from Fern's art circle, their ages ranged from about nineteen to sixty. They were all anxious to meet Mrs. Lilac, and hovered around her until it made her nervous. Mrs. Lilac knew a few of the ladies, others she had never met. They showered her with a variety of questions. Everything from politics to health. She was glad when she could get away to do personal readings; she liked it better when she could talk to people one on one.

Fern had set up a card table in her bedroom which she'd covered with a colorful pink cloth. There were several red candles lit on the dresser. The colorful touches made the readings go easily. Fern had whispered to her that she should limit them to fifteen minutes each, and that she should also limit the questions to those of romance. She tried doing that, but each of the ladies who wandered in had her own particular issue to discuss. The reading she enjoyed most was for a young girl of nineteen by the name of Barbara Cummings. Barbara was very pretty, but was dressed in a rather plain brown dress and wore little makeup. She did have a question about a boy she liked, but her most serious question had to do with whether Mrs. Lilac ever saw her moving away from home.

"My parents smother me," she told Mrs. Lilac. "My mother especially, she is extremely religious and she tries to run my life. I had to lie about where I was going tonight. Can you imagine what she would think about my having Tarot cards read? I'm not even allowed to choose my own clothes! Look at this awful outfit I'm wearing. I know I'm nineteen and should be able to be my own person, but I can't afford to go off on my own just yet. You see, I'm still in college. I have two years to go. I want to be a teacher, hopefully in the art field, but at this point I'll take whatever I can get. I just need to get away. Do you think I'll ever have a life of my own?"

"You most certainly will," Mrs. Lilac said, when she'd laid out the cards. "Not only do I see career success, but I see marriage at some point, and children. I don't think it will be to the boy you asked me about, but someone else will come along when you least expect it. Perhaps a young man, like yourself, who also needs to get away from a family who continues to clip his wings. You need to just do the best you can for now. Know that your current prison is necessary. Sometimes fences are good for us at certain times in our lives."

The girl was pleased and gave Mrs. Lilac a hug when she left. "I wish my mother was a little more like you," she said.

After that, there was a lull in the readings. There was much laughter from the other part of the house, and Mrs. Lilac assumed there was some sort of story someone was telling that had everyone's attention for the moment. To pass the time, Mrs. Lilac picked up the cards and asked her own romantic question. Would there ever be more for she and Bill Green? She shook her head as she lay out the cards, not believing she was actually doing this. Romance was never a subject she asked the cards about.

She was shocked by the answer that came to her. Friendship would turn to love. Her wish would be fulfilled. The king of cups and the ace of cups triggered a vision of she and Bill Green dancing in a garden. Great happiness would come to her, but first there would be a choice to be made. She heard one of the women coming, and she quickly picked up the cards, a rather difficult job since her hands were shaking.

When everyone had been read who wanted to be, Mrs. Lilac went back to the living room and they all had a small glass of pink champagne. Finally, Fern took the box of names, and with everyone holding their breath, she pulled out a slip of paper.

"And the painting goes to," she said in a dramatic voice, "Betty Lilac!"

There was much applause, and Mrs. Lilac felt her cheeks burn. A tear came to the corner of her eye, and she couldn't say a word as Fern handed her the painting.

"I'm glad it's going to a happy home," Fern told her, kissing her cheek.

On the way home in the car, Mrs. Lilac went back over the evening. She was thrilled to have won the painting. It had been fun and very romantic for someone who really didn't want a serious romance. At least she told herself that most days. But every time she thought of Bill Green she wasn't so sure. What could they possibly have together? Not marriage, certainly. Companionship? She would certainly be comfortable with that, sharing meals, doing fun things together. Yes, that would be exciting. But the reading she had done for herself actually indicated love for them. Was that possible? She only knew the feelings she had for him, welling beneath the surface, were more than friendship. Was it foolish of her to think that Bill Green could be feeling the same thing?

The day of the dinner date with Bill Green came more quickly than Mrs.

Lilac expected. Time just seemed to speed up, and she found herself, on the day of the event, quite nervous. She had had her hair done, and her outfit was laid out on the bed. She would be wearing a light blue pants suit with a blue print scarf. Again, she intended to go easy on the jewelry. Her short fur coat would do for a wrap.

The late February weather had turned a little chill, but the snow was nearly gone. Only a few strips and piles of it remained in the meadow. The creek bank was snow free, and in the afternoon, she took Scrappy down for a walk. Stormy seemed to be hibernating for the winter. He hated the snow, and he hated the cold. He spent most days curled up in the middle of the bed. Scrappy seemed a little upset. He had watched her earlier as she got her outfit and things together for that evening. He never liked it much when she went out and left him, and this time in particular, he was even more upset. He hardly looked at her as they went down to the stream, and this made Mrs. Lilac's heart sink. How would he ever accept moving to a new home?

She had a talk with him just before it was time for her to leave.

"Now Scrappy," she said, "I know you don't like being left alone, but it's not like I'm going to go away forever. I can't always be here with you, but you have Stormy, and Shing when she comes around. You know life isn't fair for any of us at times. But we just have to muddle through and do the best we can." She picked him up and hugged him, and he gave her a small kiss on the nose as though he understood.

Bill Green picked her up promptly at five. Once again he was dressed in his Sunday best. He seemed in a subdued mood however, and there was a kind of silence as they drove off. He had brought her a small bouquet of mixed flowers, and she took a pink rosebud and put it in the buttonhole of her jacket. It was growing dark already, and by the time they arrived at the Inn, it was pitch black. Mrs. Lilac suddenly felt a bit ill at ease. Was it the darkness, the strange place, or Bill Green's mood that she was picking up? This was not the same Bill Green who had come for Christmas dinner, nor was it the same one who had shoveled her snow only a few weeks before. There seemed to be something on his mind, and she didn't know what to say to him.

He helped her out of the car and took her arm as they went up the walk.

"You're rather quiet tonight," she said, as they neared the door. "Are you alright? You don't seem yourself."

"I'm sorry," he said. "I haven't been sleeping. It hasn't been a good month for me."

The inn had been built in 1790. It had sheltered an assorted group of famous personalities over the years, including Robert E. Lee, on his way home from Gettysburg. The rooms were filled with furniture and decor from past eras. Paintings of the Civil War hung on the wall of the dining room the were led into. A large stone fireplace was located along one wall, and their table sat nearby. The dancing fire was quite a mood setter and offered warmth in a rather chilly room.

"How lovely," Mrs. Lilac said. "This is quite a place."'

"Yes, it is," Bill Green said. "After we've eaten, the hostess will take you on a tour of the rest of it, if you'd like."

The dinner was delicious and beautifully served. Bill Green ordered steak and Mrs. Lilac had a beautiful piece of grilled haddock. The salad was unusual and quite delicious. It consisted of garden greens mixed with pieces of fruit and nuts, and was served with a house dressing.

Bill Green only picked at his food. Mrs. Lilac was beginning to feel rather low. She had expected things to go a lot more smoothly than they were going. She had thought it would be fine, even if there wasn't anything to be talked about. She had thought it would be enough to sit across from Bill, staring at his face. But tonight his face was pale and cold and showed little emotion.

Mrs. Lilac lay down her fork. She felt quite uncomfortable, but she felt she had to say something to him.

"I know you are not feeling well," she said. "Do you want to talk about it? I realize you are not yourself tonight. Would you like to go?"

She suddenly saw tears streaming down his face. He stood up. "I think we should go. I'm sorry."

Back in the car, finally, Mrs. Lilac was at a loss for words. She felt as though she could cry herself. The evening had turned into a disaster, and she had hoped for a lot more. She knew that this behavior had something to do with his wife, but it was still a terrible let down for her.

Her feelings were correct, for as they drove toward home he began to speak.

"I'm sorry I took you there, Betty," he began. "You see, it was one of my wife's favorite places. We went there many times over the years. Maybe I wanted you to be her tonight, I don't know. Maybe I thought it would all be the same and nothing would have changed. I feel I've used you in a way. I should never have believed I could go on with my life without her."

"You have not used me," Mrs Lilac said. "I know, more than anyone else, what you have been through. This is only a set back, that's all. Stop beating up on yourself. Grief takes its own course, no matter how you try to control it."

"I just know I can't do this to you anymore, Betty. You've been kind, and I don't want you to be hurt in any way."

"What hurts me," she said quietly, "Is that you are in pain. I'm not a heartless person. I do understand things, as you already know."

There was silence then, and it was not long until they were pulling into her driveway. The porch light had been left on, and she quickly started to get out of the car. Then she slid back in and looked at him. He was staring straight ahead.

"Look," she said. "I'm not upset at you in any way. I understand what has happened here. But perhaps you should know something. I've kept my feelings hidden, but I'm growing very fond of you. In fact, you've awakened something in me that I didn't even know was there. I've been acting like a schoolgirl, and I didn't think that was possible at my age. So whatever you need to do, do it. Stay away, if that's what you feel you must do. But I will always be here if you need me. So think of that for a moment and not of someone you loved who is never coming back."

She was shaking by the time she finally made it into the house. She felt as though she wanted to cry, but there were no tears. Bill Green had sat silent as she got out of the car. She knew her emotional outburst had probably dealt a death blow to whatever it was they had. But she had to say what she had said. She couldn't go on feeling what she did without letting him know. She could get through any disappointment life threw at her. What she couldn't stand was living in an emotional prison where love could not be spoken of.

MARCH

There is a feeling of expansion and expectancy as March gets underway. We have reached a place where we can see again after walking blind for so long. And what we see is a new beginning, and nothing can take our eyes from that vision.

From Mrs. Lilac's Journal.

The ringing phone woke Mrs. Lilac on a chilly March morning. Before she could pick up her bedside receiver, she heard the wind against the house and sighed. The clock on the stand read 8:05.

"Mrs. Lilac, It's Twila Marchand, do you remember me?"

Mrs. Lilac collected her thoughts before answering. Then it came back to her. The young lady she'd read for sometime in the fall. A sad relationship with a married man.

"Oh, yes of course," Mrs Lilac said. "Do forgive me, I just woke up, and my head's a bit foggy."

"I'm sorry. I didn't mean to wake you. Shall I call another time?"

"Oh no, it's fine." Mrs. Lilac said. " I'm usually awake long before now, but I was up late last night going through my things. You, see, I'm afraid I'm going to have to move in the spring and I'm trying to decide what to pack, what to throw away. I did a lot of throwing away, last night.

"I"m so sorry to hear that. It's such a nice location for you."

"Yes, I love it here, but my landlord seems to have made up his mind, and all I can do is get myself prepared."

"I was hoping I could see you, perhaps today," Twila said, after a silent pause. "A lot has happened and I'd like to run it by you."

"I'd be happy to see you," Mrs. Lilac said. "Would five o'clock work? I have someone else at six and seven."

"That would work well for me. I can't wait to see you!"

Mrs. Lilac lay in bed for a few moments just trying to clear her mind. Scrappy, lying next to her, was becoming a bit restless, and now had his head located very close to hers on the other pillow. His audible whine told her it was time to get up.

Mrs. Lilac was tired. Not only did she feel a deep ache in her muscles, she felt a deep ache of sadness in her heart. The wind outside reminded her there was a wintry forecast, and she wanted to just lie there in the warmth and safety of the bed. She had hoped that now since it was March there might be a break in the weather, and they might see Spring creeping in across the meadow. But so far, there was no such luck. The past few days had all been the same, cold with occasional snow flurries. And the wind, not a really violent wind, but a wind just the same, was harsh, and when you went outside it seemed to chill to the very soul.

She finally got out of bed and dressed. Scrappy danced around her feet, and she bundled well in her warmest coat before going out with him. They walked down to the creek bank, the cold air causing her to breathe as deeply as she could. It seemed to catch in her throat and caused a moment of coughing. Scrappy didn't seem to mind the cold, so she let go of his leash and let him wander a little by himself. She doubted he would wander far this morning.

The sky was dark, and there was no sun. The meadow was as silent as it had ever been in winter. It was as cold and empty as her own heart. And even the meadow this morning, with its wind tossed trees, seemed to hold the same kind of hopelessness that she felt inside. The stream was dark and high and ran fast before her, almost like life passing her by, and nothing could be done to stop it, only time would cause it to slow or run in a more peaceful way.

It had been more than two weeks since her dinner date with Bill Green, and much as she had tried, she couldn't get the thought of it out of her mind. If she had been one of her clients, she could have found many reasons for hope. She could even imagine what she might say to one of them, "It's a phase he's going through, he'll come out of it. He's had a set back in his grieving process." But in her own case, there was nothing she could come up with to give herself any sense of hopefulness. Bill Green was his own person, and she felt it best to step back to the boundaries of her life as they were before she had foolishly wandered across them. He was, after all, only a man she had tried to help. She had to keep it that way.

Back at the house, and out of her winter wraps, she warmed herself with a fresh cup of coffee. Then she went right back to where she had been the night before, working in the sitting room closet where years of clutter had collected. She had gone about halfway through already, and she dived in again, with just a brief thought of the attic and the outdoor shed where all the tools and the lawnmower was stored. Oh well, she thought, that's for another day. But she realized it was good to keep her mind occupied with what she was doing. That way, she wouldn't wander into uncomfortable mental areas.

By five o'clock, she was ready to see Twila Marchand. She went to no fuss in preparing for her client. She wore a simple brown sweater with a pair of slacks to match. Her psychic self seemed to have jumped out the window to escape the battle going on in her head. Better not to dress or behave as though she had anything unusual to give.

When she arrived, Twila seemed in a good mood. There was a very wide smile on her face. She was wearing a colorful green jacket and a very attractive dress in tones of green and brown.

"Well, it's over between us, Mrs. Lilac." Twila said, when they'd settled down at the table. "I did what you said, I gave him an ultimatum, and it was just as you told me. He had no intentions of leaving his wife."

"It doesn't seem to have upset you too badly." Mrs. Lilac observed. "I mean, look at you, your smile is infectious. It even gives me a ray of hope."

"Oh, it hurt me very badly at first," Twila said. "At Christmastime, I told him he had until the end of January to make up his mind. That I wouldn't wait a day beyond that. That I was tired being the other woman and could no longer live on promises."

"How did he react?" Mrs. Lilac asked.

"He threw up so many reasons why that wasn't possible that it made me tired just listening," Twila told her. "I knew then it wouldn't always be like that and I told him so. I said it was over, and I meant it. Well, he's called me every day and has sent gifts and flowers. But I have not answered his calls, and I won't. I know the way I've chosen is the right one."

"I know it is too," Mrs. Lilac said quietly. "But you'll find in time that all the sadness will lift, and you will have the happiness of a new life. Your friend will continue as he has been. He'll replace you with someone else eventually, and he'll ride that wave until it also pulls him under. His life will hold no true happiness unless, at some point, he is able to realize what is wrong. But some men never do, and can continue living forever with a wife and a mistress."

Mrs. Lilac lay down a spread of cards for her. She noticed right away that it would not be an easy reading. Not because of her client, but because of the condition of her own heart and mind. The psychic doorway seemed to be closed, the cards gave off no sparks and were only paper. But she plodded on just the same.

"It looks as though you are going to be fine, my dear." She said. "Things will gradually brighten in your life, and I think, by next year at this time, you'll have something exciting to tell me, and perhaps you will be wearing something very sparkling on one of your fingers."

Mrs. Lilac found that even in her darkest moments, some bits of information could be found in the hidden facets of the cards. She saw another man standing at Twila's doorway. He had a bouquet of flowers in his hand.

Her client smiled when she told her this. "I hope you are right, Mrs. Lilac," Twila said. "I want a marriage and children someday. I want what everyone else has!"

"No, you don't want that," Mrs. Lilac said, "You are an individual and the universe often gives us what is right for us. I do think you will get your desire, however. I do see a wedding in the future, and I think it's yours. The man at your door has a little velvet box hidden in his pocket. And there are children waiting on the pathway of your life. Two, I think. The little girl has on a lacy dress and has a little flower in her hair. Perhaps she'll come first."

When the reading was over, they sat there for a few minutes with small talk.

"You don't seem to be yourself today, Mrs. Lilac," Twila observed. "Oh, I mean I was totally happy with the reading, but the look on your face tells me something is bothering you. I think I'm a little psychic myself at times, and I can see between the layers of what is complicating things for people."

"I'm preparing to move," Mrs. Lilac told her. "I've been clearing and cleaning the house. I don't have a lot of time, and it's really worrying me."

"Are you sure this is going to happen?" Twila asked. "Maybe I can't imagine it, because you seem so comfortable here. This is your home. But I can't seem to see it."

"I wish you were right," Mrs. Lilac told her. "But I don't see my landlord backing down."

"Maybe not," Twila said. "I'm really sorry this is happening to you." She paused a moment, staring into Mrs. Lilac's face. "But there is something else bothering you, too, isn't there. If I didn't know better, I'd think you've had a heartache of some kind."

Mrs. Lilac felt tears brimming up in her eyes, and she made a great effort at stopping them. But they came nonetheless, and she had to reach for a tissue.

"You do have a strong intuition, don't you?" Mrs Lilac told her. "It's really nothing, but I allowed myself to feel something for someone, and he's pulled away from me. I didn't realize how much it would hurt, especially at my age."

"At your age!" Twila blurted out. "Love doesn't have an age or a time. It can come when we least expect it. The only bad thing is, that no matter how much joy we take from it, it can hurt all the same."

"I guess I don't see myself as a normal person," Mrs Lilac said. "It's more than just the age issue. I think I've stopped seeing myself as human. I know that is hard for you to believe, but this work I do gets to me at times. Much as I like the idea of helping others, I feel I am often expected to be God. It leaves me tired and empty."

"Sometimes all we can do is give life our best," Twila told her.

"I don't know what it is with you, young lady, but you have a way of getting into my head, and I end up telling you things I normally wouldn't tell a client."

"Well that's good," Twila told her. "What we all need at times is a friend."

"I think I've found one," Mrs Lilac told her. "You have been a dear to listen to my problems.

Now, would you like a cup of coffee?"

March continued along its path. The temperature remained chill, but at least the wind died down, and the walks to the creek bank became easier, a bit more pleasant. The sun had also come out, and she imagined she saw green everywhere. On a particular March afternoon, she was feeling a bit more relaxed and hopeful. She had just gone back to the house when a knock came to the door.

Two ladies stood on the porch who she had never seen before. At least she didn't think so. One was tall with dark hair pulled into a bun, the other a bit shorter with wavy gray hair and a very serious face. But after a second glance she realized there was something familiar in the way they stared at her.

"We'd like to talk to you," the tall one said. "I'm Glenda Starr, and this is Mrs. Cummings."

"Won't you come in," Mrs Lilac stepped aside. The pair looked at each other, nodded and then followed her into the living room. They sat on the sofa, but would not give up their coats when she offered to take them. Both of them sat there, rather stiffly, holding unto their purses as though they expected her to grab them.

"We're from the Caronsburg Lady Warriors Association," Mrs Starr said. "And we've come out here today to let you know we don't approve of you or what you are doing. Delving into the future with divination is wrong in our eyes."

"We are thinking of getting up a petition to have you put out of business," Mrs. Cummings broke in.

Suddenly, Mrs. Lilac knew where she had seen the pair before. It was in the Grill the night she and Fern had stopped in for tea after they had walked the circle at Christmas. They were the ones who had whispered about her while she and Fern had talked. She cautiously remained silent while they went on with their barrage.

"We've already talked to your landlord about you." Mrs. Starr went on. "We told him what a terrible thing for our community to have someone like yourself here so close to town."

"It seems as though you may have achieved what you set out to do," Mrs. Lilac spoke up, suddenly feeling a surge of protective energy rise in her. "He has already asked me to leave here at the end of May. And exactly what is it, beyond the card reading, that you disapprove of?"

Neither of them answered.

"Oh you don't know what it is, you just know you don't want me here. Well I have news for you, now that my landlord has done your bidding, I will be moving right into the heart of town!"

The two ladies glanced at each other, but again they had nothing more to say.

"It seems to me the two of you should have done your research before you decided to try to destroy something you didn't understand. All I have ever tried to do I s to help others. I am as God- like in my way as the both of you think you are in yours. Look around you. What did you expect to see? Dead animals and a witch's cauldron in the middle of the room? Wherever you got your preconceived ideas from, and whoever your role model was, it was not me."

Mrs. Lilac stopped a few seconds and caught her breath. She found it necessary to try harder to control her anger. This was not the first time she had encountered such unreasonable opposition, but it never failed to ire her.

" I do not live in a box." Mrs. Lilac went on. "I have a bit of Psychic ability. Where do you think it came from, Satan? No, it came partly from my ancestors who were native Americans, and partly from the experience of life. Pain and heartbreak bend and shape us, joy keeps us going, and you're trying to take that away from me. The Bible says, "Love one another," Is it love you demonstrate by trying to destroy me?"

The ladies sat there like statues. She was not sure how either of them had taken what she said, as their faces were blank. But she felt she had to change the course of what was happening.

"Now, would either of you like coffee?"

They looked at each other but didn't answer, so Mrs. Lilac went into the kitchen to prepare a tray. Scrappy had spent the visit calmly on his chair but now he approached the two ladies his tail wagging. When Mrs. Lilac brought the tray back to the living room and set it on the coffee table, Mrs. Cummings was cautiously rubbing his back.

Mrs. Lilac went to the table and picked up the cards. Somehow she felt she had to demonstrate what she did. It would either kill or cure.

She shuffled and lay out a spread, the two ladies watched her, eyes wide, faces taut and white.

"I realize you both are Christians," she said, as she laid out the cards, "and I know you believe God forgives. But what I see here is that the both of you need to forgive yourselves. One of you feels a great deal of guilt over her mother's death. It seems you weren't there for her before she died, and then she left everything she had to you." Mrs. Lilac had no idea where the facts were coming from, but they were spinning up from the unconscious and she would continue as long as the ladies listened. "One of you," she went on, "has a troublesome marriage. You have an intense desire to escape, but seem trapped by your own beliefs." The two women said nothing but Mrs. Lilac saw that both of them had tears in their eyes and their faces were flushed.

"And by the way, one of you has a beautiful daughter who will do great things with her life, but she needs a little more freedom and understanding just now. My advice to both of you is that you stop beating up on yourselves and others and learn true forgiveness."

After a moment of silence, the two ladies got up from the sofa and, without a word, let themselves out of the house. Mrs. Lilac knew she had rocked them both to the core. The bit about the daughter came when Mrs. Lilac realized the girl who talked to her at Fern's party was Mrs. Cummings daughter. It was a small world after all, and every bit of information she had in her head she would use when necessary.

Suddenly March brought rain, and Mrs. Lilac became housebound. One morning, she stood at the sitting room window and watched it come pouring down. The yard was a morass, and the creek bank was drenched with rain. It gave her a lonely, sad feeling, but if she looked closely enough, she could see hope in what lay before her. The mallards were on the stream again. They rode the swift current right before her eyes, and in a sudden flash, two of them rose into the watery sky. Robins were back. She saw two of them frisking about the wet yard. Spring was out there, and she knew it would soon come walking across the meadow. Hopefully, it would reach into her heart and plant seeds of joy. Some days, she felt as though she were being swept down the stream, in a leaking boat that would surely sink before she had her feet on solid ground again.

And then as quickly as the rain came, it stopped, and after the sky cleared, the sun was radiant and the earth began to warm. Every morning Mrs. Lilac rose to bird song and the sound of house sparrows under the eaves of the cottage. Any other year at this time, she would have been outside looking at the crocus heads lifting above the ground, or checking to see how soon the daffodils along the fence would bloom. But now, much as she wanted the new season to arrive, she was not anxious to watch the final unfolding of Spring in this spot. In the past few days, she realized more than ever, that she loved this place as much as anyone could love a place anywhere.

On a bright Friday morning, Fern called. The sun was warm, and she hadn't even needed a coat when she took Scrappy out for his walk. "I'd like to come out and give you a hand today, she said. " I know you've been busy. Perhaps I could help."

"Oh Dear," Mrs. Lilac thought, "I wish she wouldn't come out just now." But thinking ahead, she said. "Yes, perhaps we could get a little clearing done. I've gathered up a lot of clothes I no longer can wear. Maybe you could drop them off for me at one of the missions."

Fern arrived around noon. And Mrs. Lilac's spirits fell as she watched her get out of the car. She was carrying her sketching bag in one hand and what looked like a picnic lunch in the other.

"I thought it would be fun if we had a little lunch by the stream," Fern said. She seemed unusually flighty in the way she was acting, and Mrs. Lilac sighed and decided to make the most of it. She went in the house and got a checked red cloth for the table and paper plates and tableware. Scrappy was quite excited over the adventure, and even Stormy had come out of hibernation and now found the blossoming earth quite a lovely place to be out in. And what a lovely world it was. The meadow was beginning to blossom. The buds on the trees were quite evident, and all along the stream willow trees draped their fresh green branches down to the water. The cows were out again, off in the distance, and everywhere life was preparing to burst forth.

Fern had brought fried chicken, potato salad and iced tea. There were slices of cheesecake for dessert. When the table was prepared, they sat there and enjoyed the food. It was delicious, and Mrs. Lilac hadn't realized she was so hungry. When they were finished, and Scrappy and Stormy had had choice bits of the food for themselves, Fern wiped her mouth and removed her straw hat.

"Now dear," she said, "I know you are going through a hard time just now. And my real reason in coming out here today was to cheer you up and give you a little shot in the arm. You will be the same dear person I know,

105

wherever life takes you. A home is in the heart, it has nothing to do with walls or settings. Home is wherever you are."

I know you are right," Mrs. Lilac said. "But what about them," her hand indicating the pets who scurried at their feet waiting for more delicious bits. "I can't help but believe they are perfectly satisfied just where they are."

" I'm sure they are, but animals have far less trouble adjusting to new circumstances than we do." Fern told her.

"When do you think I'll be able to look at the place?" Mrs. Lilac asked. "I mean, if I don't like it I'll have to start looking again in earnest. I'm thinking about how much the rent will be, and if I can afford it."

"I spoke to Mrs. Kendall just the other day," Fern said, "She is not so much interested in making a lot of money as she is in having someone there who will take care of the place. I think it will be empty by early next month. I'm sure you can see it soon after the current tenants leave."

Mrs. Lilac left Fern there with her sketchbook and went back to the house. As she cleaned up after the picnic, she finally came to the realization that she was dragging her feet and would have to go along with the whole thing a lot more easily. Otherwise, there would be little to look forward to in her life. The universe would surely provide for her in the end. Fern was being a friend to her, and she had surprised her today, as she often did, by allowing glimpses of pure humanity come through the wacky artistic temperament that was often there.

Mrs. Lilac was preparing to go to bed that night when the phone rang. It was June Simmons.

"I"m sorry to call you so late, Mrs. Lilac," she said. "But I've got to talk to you. It's Glenn. He's acting strangely, worse than I've ever seen him. He hasn't worked in days and he stays in bed until all hours. He gets furious when I try to talk to him, and now he's mentioning suicide. It's as though he's afraid to leave the house."

You know he was here last month, don't you," Mrs. Lilac asked.

"Yes, he told me." She said. "He seems to blame all this on you. But at the same time, he seems as though he's afraid of you as well."

"I think we need to talk," Mrs Lilac told her. "We need to exchange notes. I think we may be able to get to the heart of what the real problem is. I have nothing on my slate for tomorrow. Perhaps we can get together around one o'clock."

"I'll be there," Mrs. Simmons said.

The next afternoon, when June Simmons arrived at the door, Mrs. Lilac could see at once she'd been crying.

"He's drunk," she sobbed, "and some of the things he said to me this morning were horrible. I think he's going mad!"

Mrs. Lilac led her to the sofa and offered her coffee.

"Thanks, but I don't think I could drink anything right now," she said. "I don't know how much more of this I can take."

"Let's talk about this," Mrs. Lilac said, sitting down next to her. "I want to jog your memory a little. Do you remember that first day I saw you last summer?"

"Yes, of course."

"And do you remember everything I saw in the cards that day?"

"I think so, why?"

"Do you remember when I was telling you about your mother having died? Well anyway, it was after that I saw a young girl who had died, an accident, I thought, at night?"

"Yes, I remember that. I didn't know what it meant. Why?"

"Did you ask your husband about that when you went home? You said you told him everything I talked to you about."

"Yes I did," Mrs. Simmons told her. "I did ask him about that."

"How did he react," Mrs. Lilac asked.

"His first reaction was that he didn't know what I was talking about. I do seem to remember that it sent him into a kind of quiet, introspective time, and then he asked all kinds of questions about who you were and where you lived and all that."

"Well, when he came here last month, I saw the same thing," Mrs Lilac told her. "The girl, the accident, all of it."

"Well, who do you think it is? What does it mean?"

I think it's the answer to a lot of things, but you've got to trust me, and I want you to keep our conversation private for now."

Mrs. Lilac was silent for a moment, as though weighing her words.

"Has your husband ever gone out to Mount Green Tavern? Has he ever spoken of that place?"

"He has gone there before. He used to stop there on his way home from work. Sometimes he would stay longer than others. But it's been a while since he's gone there. At least I don't remember it lately. He drinks at home these days."

"I want to make this as easy as I can," Mrs. Lilac told her. " But about two years ago a young girl by the name of Becky Wilson was killed out on

Township Road. She was the victim of a hit and run driver. It's a shortcut into town from Mount Green Tavern. I suspect your husband was the driver."

"Oh, God," Mrs Simmons said, her hand going to her heart. "Are you serious!"

"I'm completely serious." Mrs. Lilac told her. "I saw it in his cards that day he was here, but I never said a word to him. I think he was trying to figure out how much I knew. I think that was his real reason for coming to see me. He's been living with an intense sense of guilt and fear, and the thought that I might know about it seems to have nearly driven him off the edge. You see, your telling him about our reading sent him into a panic."

"Are you sure about this, Mrs. Lilac.?" Mrs. Simmons asked. "I mean, don't you think we should go to the police? If it was Glenn, I want him to face what has happened."

"I"m almost totally certain of it. I wouldn't have known about Becky Wilson, but the whole thing came to me through the readings, at a Halloween party, and later, when a client and her daughter brought me the story. It all makes sense. But there's no way as is, we can take the information to the police. They would laugh us both out of the room. The only way this thing can come to a proper conclusion is that your husband turn himself in."

"Oh, he'll never do that!" Mrs. Simmons said. "He'll kill himself before he does."

I"m not so sure." Mrs. Lilac said. "I think he will come to the point where his only option will be to go to the police on his own."

"But how can we get him to do that?" Mrs. Simmons asked. "I just don't see how it's possible."

"Well, I've been thinking," Mrs. Lilac said. "Let's turn on the heat a little. When you go home and he's sobered up and calmed down a little, tell him you came here today. But tell him we had another reading. Only this time, tell him I saw the girl again and the accident, but then tell him I said the whole thing is becoming clearer to me. That I might be able to understand it all before long."

"Do you think that's a wise thing to do, Mrs. Lilac? It sounds dangerous. Sometimes I think Glenn is capable of terrible things."

"It's the only thing I can think of that will push him into doing something about his situation. Trust me on this, please. I know you've had a hard road to travel with him. But you've come so far. If he turns himself in, and throws himself on the mercy of the courts, he will be in prison for several years, I'm sure, but in the end, he will have a chance at a life again. And that's his only hope for any kind of future for himself. As for you, you have nothing to lose. You've already come a long way, and there's no turning back."

"Okay, Mrs Lilac," she said, taking a deep breath. "We'll try this and see what happens. You know the whole thing makes sense to me, all of it."

After June Simmons left, Mrs. Lilac sat for a long time in silence. What had she done? Had she put herself in danger by going too far with the situation? She wasn't totally sure, but she did feel that what she had done was to bring a serious situation closer to a proper solution. If only a pathway through the rest of her problems were as clear in her mind. But all she could do was take one step at a time. For once, she had to take her own advice and worry only about the things in her life that she herself could control and change.

APRIL

If we can learn some lesson from heartbreak, if we can just grow the smallest bit stronger from our bad turns of fate and failure, then we can stand firm and undefeated in the face of whatever storm life might send our way. I would, if I could, stay a little while longer in April. But then there is never time enough to hold the things that we love. And it is only through traveling the circles of life that we grow and increase our values."

From Mrs. Lilac's Journal

April came, almost before Mrs. Lilac was aware that it was here. She was so busy with her concerns and her clients, that one morning she took Scrappy out for his walk, and she realized that it was unfolding before her eyes. For the first time, she saw the purple and yellow crocus in the flower bed at the front of the house and the daffodils that were ready to unfurl by the fence. And even more lovely and unbelievable, were the violets that washed across the back yard in a wide swatch. All the way down to the stream they marched before her. And dandelions, dandelions were blooming everywhere.

As Scrappy circled and foraged along the creek bank, Mrs. Lilac stared across the meadow where the grass had grown as green as spring would allow and the cows moved quietly in the distance. Her eyes followed the willows and the budding trees that lined the creek in a parade of palest green. Robins and others birds swirled along the stream, taking off and landing, crying and singing.

Mrs. Lilac breathed deeply of the scented April air. It was still a bit chilly, and she was glad for the sweater she had on. But she stood there longer than usual just taking it all in. April had always been her favorite month in this place, and for a few moments, she blanked everything else out but the beauty of all that lay before her. Yet the lines of an old story came to her suddenly, Violets are brief, and finally she came back to herself and headed back to the cottage. Scrappy was enjoying the April morning as much as she was and came reluctantly, but she didn't want to think of his unhappiness at the moment. Maybe Fern was right when she had told her that animals don't think of things in the way that people do. All she knew about animal behavior was that they showed happiness, sadness, and joy, just as humans did. It seemed no different to her as far as how they might feel about moving to a strange place. Mrs. Lilac felt they wouldn't like it anymore than she did.

Back at the house, she went to the desk in the bedroom and tried to clear up the mess. The day before, she had received an invitation to Serena and Bernie's wedding. It was almost three months away, but Rose was an extremely efficient woman. She had even included a note telling Mrs. Lilac that they were looking forward to her having a poem ready to read during the ceremony. "I'll call you in a few days to see how you are making out," she had written. Picking the note up again Mrs. Lilac's spirits sank. How could she possibly think of writing a poem for a young couple just starting out in life, when she felt like an ancient vessel from whom all hope of love had risen and escaped?

But at least she tried. On a clear sheet of paper she wrote the word Theme with a question mark. The theme would naturally be love, perhaps she could expand it from young love through the more mature love of middle age, to that of old age. No, that wouldn't be good. She was sure a young couple would not want to think of growing old on their wedding day. HOPE. That wouldn't be so bad, from LOVE to HOPE to JOY. Maybe she could do something with that. Oh, it was no use trying to come up with anything just now. Poetry had often come to her through a kind of channel from the subconscious, which usually rose on an emotional wave. This morning, even though April was working her magic on the outside, on the inside, her own emotional well had gone dry.

She was still sitting there mulling over the muddle when the phone rang. It was Fern, and she was excited.

"Dear," she said. "Could you possibly come into town today? We can take a look at the apartment. The family moved out a bit early. And Mrs Kendall would like you to see it before she calls in the painters for some freshening. I mean, so you can have a little time to make up your mind."

"I suppose I could," Mrs. Lilac said, gathering up her papers. Perhaps right after lunch. Would that work for you?"

Yes, very well," Fern said. "Don't eat anything, We'll have lunch down at the Grill, after we see the apartment.

Mrs. Lilac, a bit reluctantly, got herself together and freshened up a little before driving into town. April worked her magic all along the way, and by the time she pulled into Fern's driveway, her spirits had risen slightly.

Fern was ready and excited when Mrs. Lilac knocked on the door. She was wearing a pants suit in a wild purple color and had on a wide brimmed straw hat. Mrs. Lilac felt like a peasant in her plain gray slacks and sweater. She hadn't even bothered to wear any makeup. Fern didn't seem to notice.

"I've got the key," Fern said, coming out to greet her. "We'll just walk up there right now." Fern's street was quiet for the most part. There was a bit of traffic, but only at the busier times of day. The houses were well kept, and tulips and other annuals grew along and in front of many of them.

The house Fern led her to was a large brick one which sat rather close to the street. A brick walk went along one side and led to a door off a small stone patio. Fern put the key in the lock and opened the door. The smell of stale air greeted them as they went inside.

It took Mrs. Lilac a few moments to get her eyes adjusted to the light, but when she could finally see, her spirits sank a bit. There were five rooms in all with rather high ceilings. The living room was a nice size, but the rest of the rooms were small. The kitchen was not more than a galley, but there was a dining room, and the back door led out to a small yard with bushes and a few trees at the end. That at least made her feel better.

"What do you think?" Fern asked, taking off her hat, and leaning against the kitchen window sill. "I think you can do something with this, don't you?"

Mrs. Lilac shook her head. "I could make it into something, I'm sure," she said. "A little color and my things. I guess I have no choice. The only thing that bothers me is, will I be able to do the readings here? I can't have people complaining. And you know I need the money to survive."

"No one should complain about anything. Mrs. Kendall knows what you do, and she seems to have no qualms about it. She actually said one of her girlfriends came to you once and you helped her and gave her some good advice."

Mrs. Lilac took a moment and told her about the church ladies who had come to her door a few weeks before.

Fern shook her head. "You'd think people would have more important things to do than try to mess with you like that. But you can't let it bother you. You have a gift for helping others. You are a good, decent person."

"They actually went to Mr. Gately and asked him to have me move. Can you believe that? At least I know now why he's forcing me out."

"I don't think that's the only reason, dear," Fern told her, "I've heard for years that he's not a nice person. I'm surprised you've lived there for so long without a problem."

Mrs. Lilac walked through the rooms once again, a bit halfheartedly, before they left. She could imagine a piece of furniture here, another there. It was workable, at least, and she seemed to resign herself to the fact that she would have to do what was necessary for her survival. At least she would be close to Fern, and in many ways that would be a plus. It was one of the few reasons she could think of that would be positive about a move into town.

Back home again, though heartsick, Mrs. Lilac went on with her day as though nothing unusual had happened. After seeing to Scrappy, who was extremely glad she was back and quite ready for a short walk to the stream, she lay down across the bed and tried to rest. She had five people to read for that evening, and it was more than she cared to think about. So she lay there and tried to think of pleasant things. She thought of the April day, and her mind went to the dandelions that she had seen everywhere in such profusion. It reminded her of how, long ago, her mother had picked the plants and then cooked them and served them with a delicious dressing. She always fixed golden brown boiled and fried potatoes as a side dish. Oh, those were the good old days, and somehow the thoughts cleared her mind and she was able to rest.

When she came back to herself, she felt refreshed and the readings didn't seem so formidable. She decided to start telling her clients she would have to move. After all, she needed them to be willing to follow her no matter where she ended up.

It was nearly ten o'clock when she was finished that night. The people she talked to were sad for her, but all of them wanted to know just where she would be moving to, and that was encouraging. She felt as though she needed a cup of hot tea after everyone was gone, but Scrappy was very restless and wanted to go for his walk as soon as she was finished. He didn't seem himself tonight and barked at every corner. The stars were very bright as they walked down to the stream. Stormy made an appearance, but only momentarily, before he was off into the underbrush. She wasn't sure if Scrappy were angry at her for something or just overly excited. But he pulled at the leash and barked and barked. Perhaps some wild animal was about, a skunk, or a raccoon, as there were many of them in the woods and thickets along the stream.

In any case, she was glad to be back at the house. Scrappy settled a bit, and Stormy scratched at the door to be let in. Finally she was able to sit down with a hot cup of tea and rest her tired feet. The day had taxed her, and she hadn't realized how exhausted she was.

She was sitting there in her easy chair when Scrappy jumped up from the sofa where he was lying and started barking like a mad thing. Suddenly a loud knock sounded at the door. Mrs. Lilac felt fuzzy headed for a moment, as though she were out of focus. The knock sounded again, and her heart began to pound. What should she do? Ignore the knock and hope whoever it was would go away? The lights were all on in the house, so it was obvious she was home. At least all the blinds were shut.

Mrs. Lilac asked the universe for protection as she got up and slowly went toward the door.

"Who is it, she asked, in as loud a voice as she could muster.

"It's Glenn Simmons," the voice said angrily, "Let me in!"

Mrs. Lilac pushed back the curtain and looked out the small window. The porch light was still on, and a very angry and frantic looking Glenn Simmons stood there in the glare. He was wearing a disheveled brown jacket and his hair was wild and uncombed.

"It's late," Mrs. Lilac said calmly. "Come back another time. I'm getting ready for bed."

"I need to speak to you now," he said, in a strange, high pitched voice.

Against her better judgement, Mrs. Lilac opened the door. It was as though the subconscious had taken over, and she was acting as though some force beyond herself was suddenly in charge.

Before she could barely step aside, Glenn Simmons pushed his way into the room. Scrappy went wild and actually came rushing at the man and would have torn into him if Mrs. Lilac hadn't quickly stopped him with her foot. She reached down quickly and picked him up. Her hand rubbed his head and his bark settled down to a low growl.

"You know about me, don't you?" Glenn Simmons said loudly, his breath coming hard. "You know everything about me, isn't that right?" He moved toward her threateningly. Mrs. Lilac stood quite still and he stopped.

"I know about Rebecca Wilson," she said. "I know you're the hit and run driver who killed her."

Mrs. Lilac again had the feeling that some strange power from outside her was controlling how she felt, acted and spoke. But that was okay. Deep inside, she was just as frightened as anyone else would have been under the circumstances. Any help that was forthcoming, from the universe, from her guides, was alright with her.

Glenn Simmons stood there gasping and holding his chest. He seemed like a caged tiger who didn't know how to escape the circumstances he found himself in.

"I hate you," he spat at her suddenly. "You've ruined my life. From the moment my wife came home that day last summer, and told me about how you saw a girl who had died in an accident, I knew you would ruin everything for me. I knew it would all come to a bad end."

"I think you had better take a seat now, Mr. Simmons," Mrs. Lilac said in as calm a voice as she could muster. "I'll be happy to talk to you, but I'm not going to have you stand there like that, especially blaming me for your misfortunes."

Glenn Simmons looked around her and finally sank to the edge of the sofa. He wrung his hands as though he didn't know what to do with them. Suddenly there were tears streaming down his cheeks.

"You were the one who made those calls last Fall, weren't you," Mrs. Lilac asked, sitting down in the easy chair opposite.

"Yes," he said, a bit calmer now. "At first I had an idea in my head that you must know everything and would turn me into the police. Maybe I wanted to scare you a little. I even came out here one night to talk to you, but there was no one home. I saw you on the road, but when I came back, you were gone."

Mrs. Lilac nodded her head. That was the night she had gone into the cemetery to hide.

"And was it you in the equipment yard that night with a light?"

"Yes, that was me, too. I wanted to see your place close up. I guess around that time I had the idea then that if I did away with you that would be the end of things. But I knew I couldn't do such a thing. It was only a thought."

"No you are not a murderer," Mr. Simmons. I've known that all along. There may have been a time when I wondered, but something deep inside me made me realize you wouldn't harm me. You'd rather destroy yourself. And let's get something straight. It is not me who has caused all your problems. You don't hate me. You actually hate yourself. You are in a deep pit and you are just trying to find your way out. Your alcohol is the enemy, not me."

"I was drunk that night," Glenn Simmons said, after a long moment in which he held his head in his hands, "I guess I was speeding. But it all happened so fast. One minute I was driving along, the next I saw this wide eyed girl in the headlights. I saw her put her hand up to her face and then there was the thump. I stopped and backed up, but I panicked and got out of there fast."

"And every day since has been a hell for you," Mrs. Lilac said quietly.

Mr. Simmons nodded his head and sat there trying to keep his hands from shaking. His face looked pale and ashen, and it was as though she could look inside his soul and see the degree of torture he had put himself through.

"What do I do now?" he asked her, in a defeated voice. "What can I do to stop the pain?"

"There are only two choices," Mrs. Lilac said, rubbing Scrappy's fur with her hand. The dog had calmed down quite a bit, but still lay warily on her lap watching Mr. Simmons intently.

"You can continue on the way you are," she went on, "living with your secret, feeling guilt, anger, rage. Eventually, all of that, as well as your alcohol consumption, will kill you. Or you can do the thing you should have done from the beginning, turn yourself in. Give yourself over to the mercy of the court. You'll spend time in prison, but at least you have the hope of someday, having a life again."

"And what about my wife," he asked in a defeated voice. "I guess I've lost her, also."

"You may have lost her long ago," Mrs. Lilac said. "Will she wait for you to come out of prison? I won't answer for her, but at least you can have the peace of knowing you've done the right thing. If you are honest and hide nothing, I have a feeling the universe will help you as well. You'll be in prison, but at least you'll have a second chance someday ."

Mrs. Lilac got up then and made a pot of coffee. When it was done, she took him a large mug full. "You cannot hesitate to do what you need to do." Mrs. Lilac said, as he held the coffee and tried to steady his hands. "Go right to the station tonight. It will be a relief and a release. Will you do it?"

"I've come to the end," he said. "It's the only thing left, I guess. I would kill myself, but I don't have the courage for that. At least, I think I can do this."

They sat silently for a time. Glenn Simmons took deep gulps of his coffee and finally stood up. He didn't say another word to Mrs. Lilac. He reached out and shook her hand, and she saw that his eyes had cleared a bit. They wore a determined, resigned look. He finally mumbled goodnight and was gone.

Mrs. Lilac wandered the house for a long time that night before she could even think about trying to sleep. She couldn't help feeling sorry for Glenn Simmons, but she was glad his ordeal could now come to some sort of conclusion, painful as it might be. But he could have made it a lot easier on himself. What really struck her, and what was so hard for her to let go of, was the fact that she was often so misunderstood. Yes, she knew she had psychic abilities, but she certainly did not know all the things people thought she did. Glenn Simmons had assumed so much about her, had obviously suffered a great deal thinking she knew, from the very beginning, who he was and what he had done. And while his suffering was of his own making, and had gone on and on due to shame and cowardice, she hoped he would, this very night, do the right thing and bring the whole matter to a kind of end.

Finally, her nerves calmed enough for her to go to bed. Sleep, however, would not come. She was in a half doze when she heard a familiar scratching at the window. She sighed and got up and after a bit of fumbling was able to open the stubborn thing.

"I hope you realize, Shing," she said to the silence, "that I've had a very difficult night."

But then she smiled and took a deep gulp of April air. It was quite a bit chilly, but she decided to leave the window open a crack. Perhaps dear Shing just wanted to comfort her in some way, perhaps she understood some of the deeper areas of her psyche that were bothering her.

She finally dozed off, after thinking that the whole world probably thought she was crazy, but so be it.

A ringing phone woke her suddenly. Light was streaming in the window, and the bedside clock said it was eight thirty. Mrs. Lilac fumbled for the receiver.

Hello," she said, her mind still in a fog.

"Mrs. Lilac? It's June Simmons." The voice was high pitched, excited. " I'm sorry I'm calling so early, but I wanted you to know. Glenn turned himself in last night. I got a call at an early hour from the sheriff. There is no bail, but I am going to get in touch with our attorney. At least he deserves legal advice, and you know I do feel sorry for him."

"Of course, you do, dear," Mrs. Lilac said. "You didn't want things to turn out the way they have. Your husband made his own choices, and now he will have to take responsibility for them. He was here last night, you know."

"No, I didn't know about that."

"Yes, he came here, as I thought he would. And he admitted the whole thing. I really believe he had come to the end of his rope. I told him there was only one way out for him. I want you to believe, that by his taking this step, he has given himself another chance at life."

"I know, Mrs. Lilac." She said. "And I want you to know, I'll never be able to thank you for being there when I needed someone. I think it's too late for Glenn and I, but at least we both can now look ahead to a fresh start. That's all I can hope for, for him and for myself."

Mrs. Lilac finally hung up the phone and slid out of the bed. A weight seemed to have been removed from her body, and she dressed hurriedly.

Scrappy was circling around her feet, and before she'd even had a chance to make coffee, she had to go out with him into the April morning.

Already, the grass was getting a bit high, and she realized, that before long, she would have to call David to come mow for her. And that thought brought her mind back to Bill Green. It had been nearly two months since the disastrous dinner at the inn, but there was a sad feeling when she thought of him. If only things had turned out differently. At least she wished that they could have remained friends.

The phone didn't seem to want to stop that day. One client after another seeking advice, wanting to come see her. In the afternoon, she heard a familiar voice when she lifted the receiver.

"It's Joanne Barkely, the voice said, remember me, the Feather Lady?"

"Of course, I remember you, Mrs. Lilac said.

"Mrs. Lilac, you were so right about Becky Wilson. You said we would soon know who it was who killed her that night. It's all in the paper today. The person who did it turned himself in. Someone by the name of Simmons. Have you heard?"

Yes, dear," I have," Mrs. Lilac told her. "It's a long story. But I'm glad the whole thing is going to be settled soon. I'm sure your daughter will be able to put this behind her now."

"Yes, she's quite relieved," Joanne told her. "Sad of course, but still glad at least that this may bring a kind of closure. It won't bring her friend back, but perhaps she can live with things more easily."

"Life is really strange at times," Mrs. Lilac said, brushing at an invisible piece of lint on her dress. "But I have always felt that the universe is fair. Let's pray that something tragic can work for good in those who are left. Becky is in a world of joy and light. And when we go back to that place, there is no questioning how we got there. We just know there is no other place we'd rather be."

Before she knew it, Easter began to emerge from the dark of the past difficult weeks. She invited Fern for dinner, and then thought it might be nice to have Wanda and Julie come also.

They would certainly liven things up, and if ever there was a time when she needed enlivened, it was now. She remembered their antics at Christmastime and it made her smile. But as she was making the notes for what the dinner might consist of, ham, sweet potatoes, cole slaw, she realized she would have to break the news to the girls that this would probably be their last visit to see her at the cottage. This sobered the rest of her note taking, and by the time she was ready to makes the calls to her friends, she wondered if having anyone for the holiday was really a good thing.

But the plans went forward in spite of her misgivings, and Easter Day dawned bright and beautiful. Mrs. Lilac went out quite early with Scrappy and Stormy to the creek bank. The sun was rising over the meadow, and it was quite a spectacle to behold. The scent of the green earth brought tears to her eyes. She took in the look of April, the pale green, the awakening earth, the golden daffodils, for soon it would be gone, and the passing of no other season bothered her quite the way it did when April was gone over the hill. But she said a prayer to the universe for help and guidance, and also for protection for herself and the pets. There would be life beyond April. There would be life beyond the cottage and the creek bank. She would have to be satisfied with the idea that this place, the years of her life here, this morning, this moment, would always live in her heart.

Fern was the first to arrive, just after eleven o'clock. She seemed a bit more toned down, if such a thing were possible. She had on a pair of pink slacks with a sweater to match. She also wore her usual painter's straw hat and a large pair of sun glasses. For some reason, Mrs. Lilac had the feeling she was running smoothly on all her mental cylinders today. She was glad Fern hadn't worn an elaborate outfit for the holiday, as she herself was dressed in plain gray slacks with a light blue sweat shirt. Since she would be busy with the food, she hadn't felt like dressing up in any way.

"Beautiful day, isn't it dear?" Fern said, handing Mrs. Lilac a small crystal basket in which were nested three beautifully decorated miniature eggs.

"Oh, thank you! Isn't this lovely. You shouldn't have brought me anything though," Mrs. Lilac told her. "I thought we'd just keep things rather simple today. Dinner is nearly ready. You can help me a bit when it's time. Before the girls come, let's just sit here quietly and have some coffee."

"Great idea," Fern said, " I was busy all day yesterday with an Art show. And do you know, for the first time in years, I won only an honorable mention with one of my oils."

"That's too bad," Mrs Lilac said. "But next year is another year, and your luck will come around again. Remember that."

"And your luck will change, too," Fern told her. "You know, I lay awake a long time last night thinking about you and all that you've had on your plate the last few months. I finally saw everything clearly, and I want you to know, I understand, even if I act like I don't sometimes, even if it seems I don't have a brain in my head."

They were sitting there quietly a few moments later when Mrs. Lilac heard the sound of a car in the driveway. A door slammed, and there was loud laughter from the front porch.

Of course it was Wanda and Julie. Once again, the two of them had outdone themselves. Mrs. Lilac opened the door to find them dressed as Easter rabbits. Wanda was blue, Julie was pink. The outfits were complete from the tall ears to the fluffy tail at the back. There was just enough room for their faces. The two of them turned like gyros so Mrs. Lilac could get the complete view. All the time they were laughing hysterically, and Mrs. Lilac had to hold unto the edge of the door to keep herself from losing it. Both the girls carried a large Easter basket filled with a virtual potpourri of various eggs and rabbits and an assortment of other colorful, unknown objects.

"We're the Easter rabbit twins," Wanda said. "We decided to come dressed for the occasion."

"Fern came to the door to see what the hubbub was all about. She covered her mouth and began to chuckle. Fern knew the two girls from past social events, but had never seen them in all their glory as Mrs. Lilac had. It was certainly going to be an interesting day.

As usual, the two girls had gifts for every one. There was a chocolate rabbit and egg, plus other assorted candies for Mrs. Lilac and Fern. And as for the pets, there were plush rabbits and biscuits for both.

"Where did you get the fabulous outfits?" Fern asked, shaking her head.

"The girls quieted down enough to answer. By this time they were all settled in the living room.

"Wanda does the Easter egg hunt each year for the kids at the hospital," Julie told them. "She has all the employee's children, and each year there are more and more, so we decided last year that two rabbits would be better than one. We just had the event yesterday, so we thought it would be a fun idea to come dressed for dinner in character."

"Yes," Wanda, broke in, "We decided to give Mrs. Lilac a good laugh since she hasn't had one since we were here at Christmas."

The two girls broke into hysterical laughter. Mrs. Lilac wondered if it was always like that for them. It must be quite an accomplishment to find so much joy in such simple things. She admired the girls for that. She was glad she had invited them, though she wasn't sure how they would take her news.

At least the dinner went beautifully. The ham was tasty and tender, and all the extras were delicious. Wanda and Julie ate heartily, and even Fern, who usually ate like a bird, really dived in and had a second helping of everything. For dessert, Mrs. Lilac had fixed a banana cream pie, and everyone raved about it. Even the twin rabbits were filled to the ears when they were finished with the meal. They sat around for a while with cups of hot coffee until Wanda and Julie finally jumped up and started rooting in one of the baskets.

"We've brought jelly beans for the Goddess," Julie said, holding a plastic bag of colorful candy out for them to see.

"And a couple of hard boiled eggs," Wanda said. "I'm sure she won't mind when they break open and the fish get a treat. Come on, we all have to go down to the stream!"

Mrs. Lilac's heart wasn't in it. She could tell by Fern's reaction that she thought they were all crazy, but they got up and followed the two girls, still costumed to the max, down to Rainbow River.

The afternoon sun was down low in the sky by this time, but the air had warmed a bit and the scents rolling in from the meadow were indescribable. The pale green of the trees and the bushes was a perfect feast for the eye.

"I wish I had my painting things with me," Fern said, her eyes on the meadow. "This is just a beautiful scene."

It is, isn't it," Mrs. Lilac said, and tears started to fill her eyes. Partly because she had had a lot to do to get ready for the day, and was quite exhausted, but mostly because of the thought that it would be her last April here to view the world coming alive.

Wanda noticed her tears and rushed to her side. "What's wrong, Mrs. Lilac? Are you sure you are feeling okay?" Wanda was a nurse and always seemed to be watching for any sign of ill health in whoever she was with.

"I'm okay," Mrs Lilac said, wiping at her eyes. "I guess I was just thinking ahead, and I haven't told you or Julie what is happening. You see, I have to move. My landlord insists. I won't be here beyond the last part of May."

The two girls stopped dead in their tracks for a moment, almost like tableaux, before bursting into tears. Both of them had streams of liquid running down their cheeks and unto their colorful costumes.

"Why, what's happened?" they both spoke the same words at once. "Why do you have to move?" They had always had the habit of knowing what each other was thinking and often ended up speaking the thought at the same time.

Mrs. Lilac told them the story. She finally assured them that she would still be around, but that her home would now be at the center of town.

"But what about the stream?" Julie said. "What about the Goddess? Who will bring her things, like jelly beans and eggs?"

"Like sticks and stones and beer?" Wanda piped in.

"Girls," Mrs. Lilac said. "Don't forget that we have created the Goddess. She lives in our imaginations and in our spirits. We can give her offerings wherever we are. We must remember this."

The two girls finally sat at the picnic table where Mrs. Lilac and Fern had taken refuge. For several moments they all huddled there in a kind of dejected mood. Mrs. Lilac had never seen two more depressed rabbits. Both of them had tear stained cheeks and even their ears drooped. Then, nearly in the same motion, the two of them stood up and quickly walked to the edge of the stream. Julie took a handful of jelly beans and tossed them in one direction, creating a momentary rainbow of color. Wanda threw a handful in the other, the pieces of candy making pattering sounds as they landed on the surface. Scrappy had gone to the bank with the girls, and he pranced and barked as the beans hit the water. Then each one of them threw a colorful hard boiled egg into the center of the stream where they were standing. There were two loud plops and then silence.

"Come on, Mrs. Lilac," they called, "there are more here for you to throw. Fern, you too, come throw some candy into the stream for the Goddess."

"I don't think so this time, girls," Mrs. Lilac said. Fern also declined with a shake of her head.

"The Goddess will understand," Julie said finally, coming back to the table. "I know she feels your pain. Perhaps she'll intervene for you in some way."

"You have more faith in her than I do," Mrs. Lilac said. "I hope she'll forgive me for that."

"I know she'll be with you wherever you are, Wanda said, coming up to give her a gentle hug.

"Because you know what, Mrs. Lilac, you're the real Goddess, and as long as you are alive, she is."

"She'll always be in your heart," Julie said, bursting into tears again. "And you'll always be in ours."

Batty as bedbugs, Mrs. Lilac thought, but so kind and human. She was glad the two of them were in her life. She hugged them one by one and then together.

April had only a few days left to go. It was Saturday afternoon and Mrs. Lilac was finished with all that the day had given her to do. The empty picnic table made her think of the Easter dinner and of a sad Wanda and Julie, but that was behind her now.

The lilacs were now in full bloom. She sat looking back to where her own bushes bloomed profusely as the edge of the yard. There were both purple and white ones and a darker purple that was so beautiful it was almost indescribable. She had already picked two bouquets for the house, and several of the clients had brought her small bunches of flowers. Her name, of course, had actually come from the clients, who, every spring, found the cottage full of the colorful blossoms, and over and over greeted her with the name Mrs. Lilac. And over the years it stuck. Her mother loved lilacs also, and Mrs. Lilac would always put the largest bouquet she could gather on the oak buffet in memory of her. She remembered the time when she was a girl, and she and her mother had gone into the countryside to gather lilacs. They had come to a literal grove of the blossoming bushes and had picked two huge armfuls, when they discovered they were standing in an overgrown graveyard.

"Don't worry, Betty. The residents won't mind." Her mother had said. " They probably enjoy having visitors."

Mrs. Lilac smiled to herself remembering that long ago day. Time was like a carousel, she realized, it took everything lovely away but brought it back and back again as memory.

She was standing there, ready to go back to the house, when Scrappy began barking loudly. She turned in the direction of the cottage and was stunned to see Bill Green coming toward her down the slope. He was dressed in his green work clothes and had a huge bouquet of purple lilacs in his arms.

She felt like a statue suddenly and couldn't move. Her body felt as though it were jelly, and she wished she had something to hold on to. She wrapped Scrappy's leash very tightly around her arm, as though that would help. Scrappy stood up on his hind legs as Bill Green came up to where she was standing.

For a moment, neither of them spoke. Mrs. Lilac was aware of her heart pounding in her chest.

"I brought these for you," Bill Green said, finally. "They're blooming everywhere down home, and I thought it would be a shame if they all went to waste."

"Thank you," Mrs. Lilac said, after a moment of silence. "They're beautiful. Perhaps you can carry them back to the house for me. I'll put them in the center of the table."

He followed her to the house and stood there looking on while she found a large enough vase, and then transferred the huge bouquet from the kitchen sink to the living room table.

The scent of the blossoms, along with those that were already there, had permeated the whole house with a magnificent perfume.

"Please sit down," Mrs. Lilac finally said. "Won't you stay awhile?"

Bill Green silently slid to a place on the sofa, and Mrs. Lilac brought him a cup of hot coffee and a slice of lemon pound cake. Then she sat opposite him in the easy chair.

He ate the cake silently and then lay down the fork and looked at her.

"I owe you an apology," he said, carefully weighing his words. "You don't know how many times I've wanted to come and talk to you since that night we went to the Inn, but I just couldn't do it. You see, I was ashamed and embarrassed. I never should have taken you to that place. It was my wife's favorite restaurant. Perhaps I was trying to recreate the past, perhaps I was trying to test myself, I don't know, but it didn't work. It was indeed a setback, as you said, and I had a hard time coping with it. I thought, for a time, that I should just stay alone and forget the idea of coming back into life again. Now I realize that was wrong. I need to be with people. And... and.. I missed you."

"I missed you, too," Mrs Lilac told him, when he stopped for a moment to take a sip of coffee. "And I understand, more than you know. It was so sad for me to see you like that, knowing there was nothing I could do, knowing that words sometimes seem such empty things, but in the end they are all that we have."

"I picked a lot of morel mushrooms at the beginning of the month," Bill went on, "and I wanted to bring you some. But I didn't get up the courage. Have you ever tasted morels, Betty?"

"Oh yes," she told him. "I used to pick them when I was a girl. My mother loved them. I wish you had brought me some. We used to dip them in flour and brown them in olive oil. I can almost taste them now."

"I'll be sure that you get some next year, Betty. I hope there will be a next year for us."

"Of course, there will be," she told him. "Nothing has changed. You're forgiven for whatever you think you've done to hurt me. I want us to be friends again. I really do. Do you think that we can be?"

Yes, I'm sure of it," he said, and the look he gave her, a look of sadness but one of joy and hope at the same time, melted something dark that had been wrapped around her spirit for too long.

After he'd gone, Mrs. Lilac stood on the porch in the late afternoon light. Scrappy sat beside her looking down the road where Bill Green's truck had disappeared. Once again he had worked some kind of magic within her. The universe had given her a gift and a boost when she needed it most. All around her the hope of the blossoming world seemed to settle. Violets are brief, she thought. Perhaps April is nearly over, but like first love, we will remember her always.

MAY

Time moves so smoothly from April into May it is impossible to tell where the transition was made. Any sorrow at April's passing is eased by the warm and softening air, the greening land and the millions of blossoms.

From Mrs. Lilac's Journal

It was the first Saturday in May, and Mrs. Lilac awoke to the sound of the mower outside her bedroom window. Scrappy was already off the bed and barking his head off. Looking out the window, Mrs. Lilac saw David moving back and forth at the bottom of the yard. She dressed quickly and was in the kitchen making coffee when he came to the door and knocked.

"I'll take Scrappy out for you," he said when she opened the door. "Hope I didn't wake you.

"I'm glad you did," she told him cheerily. "I need to be up and about. Have you had breakfast?"

"I grabbed some cookies," he said.

"You can't live on cookies," she told him. "I'll fix you some eggs and bacon. And how about some orange juice?"

"Hey, that sound's great," he said.

By the time the mowing was finished, Mrs. Lilac had the pine kitchen table set with her blue willow plates. The lilacs were still blooming, though they were fading now, but she had managed to fix a nice bouquet for the center of the table.

"Wow, Mrs. Barnes, this looks nice." David said, when he came in from the yard. "You didn't have to go to all this trouble. Paper plates would have been fine."

"It's no trouble, and besides, you're special," she told him.

"No, I'm not," he said, grinning sheepishly. "But I know someone who thinks you are. I spoke to Bill Green the other day, and his face was all smiles when we talked a little about you."

Mrs. Lilac was sure she was blushing, but she just grinned and lowered her eyes.

"In fact, I think he's acting like someone who's falling, you know, like in love."

"David! I'm sure you're just exaggerating." Mrs. Lilac protested. "He's doing better, I think, he's trying to move on with his life. I doubt very seriously if it has much to do with me. I just helped him a bit, that's all."

"Yeah, well, you didn't hear it from me, but something's putting a bit of a sparkle in his eye these days, and I'm sure it's not his cows."

Later, Mrs. Lilac stood on the porch and shook her head and watched David's truck move off down the road. "That boy!" she thought, always trying to cheer her up with his teasing, and as embarrassed as he made her, she was always glad when he came to see to her chores or just for a friendly visit.

There were no clients that afternoon, so when she was finished with household chores, Mrs. Lilac sat down at her desk and tried to concentrate on the poem she was writing for Serena and Bernie's wedding. Rose had called her a couple of days ago to ask how she was doing, and she didn't have the heart to tell her that she hadn't set down a single line. So now she had to concentrate. From the desk, she could see how beautiful the May landscape had become. The scent of the newly mown grass drifted in where she had raised the window a crack. After Bill Green's visit a few days before, and David's fresh mentioning of him this morning, Mrs. Lilac's heart felt a little more inclined to think on the subject of love. At least about the sorts of things one would write for a wedding poem. Some lines came to her mind and she picked up her pen.

"Dear ones at this special gathering,
With my heart on this joyful day,
may love be there for you always,
Along all of your way..."

Mrs. Lilac felt a bit better that a few words had bubbled up in her, and she was just ready to grasp another line when Scrappy began barking again, and a knock came to the door.

When she went to see who it was, she was a bit shocked to find Mr. Gately standing there. He was dressed in slacks and a sweater, not the work dress she was used to seeing him in. His face was sober and dark, and she still acted as though nothing had happened and invited him in.

It seemed something was bothering him, but he shook his head and stood silently for a moment. "I just wanted to know if you realized your lease is up at the end of the month."

Anger rose in Mrs. Lilac. How in the world could this man think she had forgotten his summer visit? How could he think her world had gone on in such a way that she could forget it was nearly time for her to end a major part of her life in this place?

The words came out of her and it was as though she couldn't stop them.

"How in the world do you think I couldn't know that? You are obviously not a caring or sensitive man, otherwise you would know the pain and suffering your last visit caused me. For months, I have agonized over your decision to have me leave here, and I am getting ready to go. But whether or not I will be out at the end of the month is another story. It may be a few days longer, it may be a month, but I will be out. If you find you need to have an eviction notice sent, that's perfectly fine. But I can't end twenty years of a life on a certain day just because my landlord thinks I should."

Mr. Gately seemed shocked by her outburst. He stood stock still and looked over her head.

"And by the way," she went on, "those church ladies were here and gave me their spiel about my being evil and all that, and I just wanted you to know they told me they had come to see you. It would have been nice if you could have let me know. So I'll say the same thing to you I said to them. I am a kind and generous woman. Every night I agonize over the suffering of humanity. I have tried to help others and give comfort where I can. And your decision to separate me from a place I have loved with all my heart, may cause me pain for awhile, but it will not destroy me. I will live on despite you and your selfish decision. Now I bid you good day."

Mrs. Lilac slammed the door. She sat down on the sofa for a moment trying to get herself together. Her heart was beating at a frightening rate, but her arms were still attached, she still felt her toes. She knew that when anger rose in her, it sometimes came like a flood, and it could destroy everything in its path, including her. Finally, after a short time, she felt herself sink back to normal, and was aware of the clock ticking, and of the birds still singing outside the window. And looking down, she saw Scrappy staring up at her, his tail wagging. He seemed to be telling her it was time for a walk.

She attached his leash, and they went out into the afternoon light. There was no sign of Mr. Gately. Stormy actually came with them this time, and Mrs. Lilac decided she needed more of a walk this time, and perhaps the exercise would clear her mind. It had been a few weeks since they had gone into the storage yard, and somehow that's where she wanted to be just now.

There were no workers about since it was late Saturday, and the dirt track led them through an enchanted world. The hulks of the old machinery were covered by green vines. In a few weeks there would be wild roses blooming, and the honeysuckle scent would waft across the air, but just now, there were various wild flowers blooming and birds flew everywhere. Scrappy was more interested in where the next rabbit would make its appearance than he was in what Mrs. Lilac was thinking. And what she was thinking was that there was nothing left for her to fear. Was it the splendid landscape of May, the more mature twin of April? Was it the fact that she had finally said what she had always wanted to say to Mr. Gately, or was it that somehow the blockage of the past months had finally given way, and she could see clearly again after so long a time? She didn't know, but a strength of spirit seemed to have risen up in her and her heart was filled with praise. Praise for the universal spirit that had kept her safe for so long, praise to the natural world that soothed her spirit at this moment. She concentrated the rest of the walk on the amazingly soft heads of the trees that were bursting forth bit by bit, day by day. The willows along the stream were as pale green as fresh green could be.

They finally made it back to the cottage, and Mrs. Lilac was stunned to see Mr. Gately's truck sitting in her driveway. Mr. Gately was still inside.

What more could he possibly want to say to her now? She raised her mental barbs for battle, but passed the truck without looking at him. She was getting ready to go inside when she heard him step out of the truck and shut the door. Turning round, she waited until he hurried up to her.

He seemed out of breath, and his eyes were red as though he'd been crying. Mrs. Lilac couldn't believe the kind of broken man who stood before her.

"I need to speak to you a moment," he said, excitedly. "and it's not about your moving. I wanted to talk to you before, but I lost my nerve. And then, just a few moments ago, I got the latest call from the hospital. So I felt I had to come back."

"Come inside," Mrs. Lilac said. She pushed open the door and stepped back while he entered. Stormy rushed past them and ran into the bedroom. She was surprised that Scrappy hadn't shown any signs of aggression, but instead was wagging his tail and whining for attention.

"Please sit down," Mrs. Lilac said, indicating the easy chair.

Mr. Gately sat, and Mrs. Lilac sank down on the sofa.

"It's my wife," Mr. Gately, began, his voice high pitched and shaky. "She's been ill for some time. Right now she's in the Central State hospital. I just got a call from there and they said to come right away. She's dying."

"Oh my," Mrs. Lilac said. "What is it, what happened?"

"She had heart surgery yesterday, quadruple bypass and valve repair. It was a risky surgery to begin with, because she hasn't been well, and I finally agreed to it because I didn't have a choice." Mr. Gately choked up and put his hands to his eyes. Mrs. Lilac quickly got up and handed him a tissue.

"Well, there is internal bleeding, and they can't seem to get it stopped. She's had transfusion after transfusion, and I think they've given up on her. They called in the priest, and I'm on my way there. You were my last hope. Do you think there is any chance for her?" He was crying now, and Mrs. Lilac forgot her earlier anger. She only saw him as she saw any of her clients, someone who needed a bit of light in a dark situation. She got up from the chair and went to the table. She didn't even take the time to have Mr. Gately shuffle the cards. She shuffled them herself and quickly lay down a spread.

The cards were a mixed bag. The Tower at the center was a bad omen, but it could represent the current situation. The World in the final outcome position could mean a release for Mrs. Gately, even death, but it also could mean recovery. She followed the path of the cards and images began to come to her.

"It is a grave situation," Mrs. Lilac began, "and I think you are right. Her doctors do seem to have given up. Your wife is weak, frail. But I don't see death. This can be turned around. At the darkest moment there appears to be light. Mr. Gately, I want you to pull yourself together now. Be as firm and as strong as you can be. I want you to go back to the hospital and speak to her doctors. You must be insistent that they not stop the transfusions. Serious as this is, I think your wife can recover. But you must be firm about it. And you don't have any time to waste."

Mr. Gately got up from the sofa like a shot and headed toward the door. She heard the words "Thank You," come back over his shoulder, and then from outside there were the sounds of squealing tires as Mr. Gately's truck headed up the road at a high rate of speed.

It took Mrs. Lilac a few minutes to pull herself together after her strange encounter. She sat there and thought back to the winter when she had run into Mr. Gately and his wife at the market. No wonder she had looked so ill. She shook her head, thinking of how she had gone off at Mr. Gately earlier. But it was his fault as well. Why hadn't he just come out and told her what was bothering him? She was a very forgiving woman, but she also knew how to stand up for herself when she felt backed into a corner.

Early the next week she had a phone call from Rose Wilder. "Mrs Lilac," she said excitedly. "Serena and I want to come for a reading if you can work us in this week. Things are already getting hectic and beyond this we won't have much time. There's so much going on and we want to see what things look like for the wedding. And how is the poem coming?"

"Actually not bad," Mrs. Lilac told her. "I have it started and seem to know the direction it is going in. Perhaps I can finish it before you come. Then you can decide if it's good enough."

"Oh, don't worry if it's good enough. It will be from you, and that's all that matters."

They sat up an appointment for later that week, and Mrs. Lilac, when she had some free time, sat down at the desk and looked over what she had already written. It was afternoon and the scents of the season wafted in the open window.

Deep in the sky at twilight,
On the brightest day or the darkest night,
In a million stars glittering above you,
Pledge to keep love safe and bright....

She had stopped there, and took the poem up again at that point. Her mind seemed more open now, and before she knew it, she was writing the last lines,

May love live for you then and forever,
that is my wish, this is my gift.

She gave a sigh of relief. It would have to be revised a bit, but that was the best she could do. Perhaps someone would think it a bit trite, but she had written it from her heart and that was all that mattered.

She had no sooner got up from her desk when she heard Scrappy's shrill bark and another knock at the door.

"What now?" she wondered, It seemed there was never enough time in the day to do all the things she needed to do for herself.

It was Annabelle Wilkins. But it didn't look like Annabelle. She was dressed in a dark gray suit with a wide skirt and had on plain walking shoes. Her salt and pepper hair was pulled into a tight bun at the back of her neck. The dread locks were gone, as was the hat and basket. The purse was a plain gray bag over one arm. Her face was taut and showed a sad look.

"Annabelle," Mrs. Lilac said, a bit shocked. "Is that you?"

"It's me, honey, it's me." Annabelle said, "Can this poor tired woman come in?"

"Of course, dear, come in and rest a while. Did you walk all the way out here again?"

"I did honey, I needed to do something." she said in a tired voice. "The exercise does me good. I'm getting on a bus this evening. I'm goin' back to Mississippi, you see, and I wanted to see you before I went."

"Annabelle, what's happened?" Mrs. Lilac asked, as she ushered her into the living room and helped her get seated on the sofa. "Your sister..."

"I lost her, honey," Annabelle said, tears welling up in her eyes. "She just got tired and didn't want to go on no longer. Oh, I tried, but sometimes tryin' ain't enough. I gave it all I had. I worked so hard to keep her goin', but all the herbs and weeds and spells and deeds, won't keep someone here when they are ready to go back home..."

I'm so sorry Annabelle." Mrs Lilac told her. "I don't take the local paper, so I'm not always aware of what is happening."

"It's okay, honey. A lot of people don't know yet."

Mrs. Lilac fixed her a cup of hot tea and brought a plate of sugar cookies to the coffee table, but Annabelle didn't touch them. She did manage to sip at the tea.

"So I decided to go back home myself for awhile." Annabelle went on. "Oh, I know I'll hate it there after awhile, but I gotta see to some things and visit a few people, and then I'm gonna put my feet up and just sit still for awhile."

"Do you think you might come back here at some time?" Mrs. Lilac asked. "We'll miss you, you know."

"And I will surely miss you, honey." Annabelle said, fussing with her tea cup. "You are one of the bright spots in Caronsburg. And there ain't many bright spots in this town. And I need some light to see where I'm headed, deed I do. But I won't say, no, never, to anything. The stream of life moves, and Annabelle goes with the flow."

"Well, please send me a post card from time to time." Mrs. Lilac told her. "Hopefully the post office will send it on to me."

"Honey you ain't goin' nowhere." Annabelle insisted. "I took care of that old landlord of yours. You gonna be in this cottage till the day you die. I'm sure of that."

"No, I'm afraid you're wrong, Annabelle. This is my last month here, at least my last legal one."

Annabelle just smiled and reached into her bag. She pulled out an object and held it in Mrs. Lilac's direction. "I found this one day walkin' in an empty lot behind the house. I thought about you when I first saw it, and I'm givin' it to you as a kind of good luck piece."

131

Mrs. Lilac took the object and help it in her hand. It was a flat rock, gray in color with streaks of crystal running through it. It was in the crude shape of a heart.

"That's for luck and love, honey," Annabelle said, her voice taking on a lighter note. "Because that's what I'm wishin' for you. That's what I'm wishin' for you."

When she was ready to leave, Mrs. Lilac offered to drive her into town, but Annabelle refused to think about it. "No, Honey," she said, "I need the exercise, cause I'll be sittin' on my bottom on that old bus for the next couple of days."

When she got up to leave, Mrs. Lilac hugged her fondly. She felt tears in her eyes, but tried to control them for Annabelle's sake.

"If I don't see you in this world, I'll see you in the next." Mrs. Lilac told her. "Thanks for all your kindness to me,"

"And you too, honey," Annabelle's voice trembled. "I won't forget you."

Mrs. Lilac watched at the window until she was out of sight, a tall figure walking into the sun. She shook her head. So many changes everywhere, every day. One never knew what was around the next turn. She only knew that whatever life brought her she would rise to the occasion. Perhaps not always so willingly, but rise, she would. She said a silent prayer that the universe would keep Annabelle safe on her journey.

A few days later Rose and Serena came for their reading. This time they all sat at the table together. Rose was more animated than Mrs. Lilac had ever seen her, and Serena, in spite of all that she had with school exams and everything else, seemed actually serene.

"I think I'm going to fall apart," Rose said, her voice high-pitched. "Thank God, I will never have to totally plan another wedding."

"Oh, come on," Serena chided. "I'm the one who should be falling apart here. It's me who has the weight of the world on my shoulders, what with final exams and all, and just trying to put up with you!"

"Mrs. Lilac," Rose said, totally changing the subject. "Serena and I were talking. Of course you should wear anything you'd like for the wedding, but we'd like to see you in a purple or lilac colored frock, with shoes and hat to match. What do you think?"

"Well, I actually have a lovely purple dress and jacket outfit which I think would do fine. But as for shoes and hat, I think I will have to do a bit of shopping."

"Wonderful," Serena said excitedly, "and I see you in a kind of broad brimmed hat. None of those small little lacy things for you. What do you think, mother?"

"That sounds great," Rose said. "And what about the poem, Mrs. Lilac. Is it finished?"

Mrs. Lilac reluctantly went to the bedroom and brought back her simple creation. She felt a little awkward as she handed it to Rose. What if they didn't like it?

"Why its lovely," Rose exclaimed, after reading hurriedly down the page. "It sets just the right tone, and I can see you standing there on the stage reading it."

Serena concurred that her poem was beautifully written. "It's just what I'd hoped it would be," she said. "What we're going to do is have four speakers who will come in from the side, do their thing, then remain on the stage for the actual ceremony. You'll be the last to come on, Mrs. Lilac, and then you'll be right up there when we get married."

"Oh my," Mrs. Lilac said, suddenly feeling a large dose of anticipatory anxiety. "Do you think I can really do this? I"m already seeing myself standing there in a panic, unable to speak."

"You'll be fine," the two of them said, almost at once, but Mrs. Lilac felt it very difficult to concentrate after that. How many years had it been since she'd actually stood on a stage, and spoke in front of a large audience? Years, indeed. But she tried to keep her mind on the cards when they were finally laid out.

"I don't see any major snafues," she told them. " In fact, it looks as though everything will go beautifully. Even the weather will cooperate. And I see flowers, flowers, everywhere."

"We're going to have a virtual garden recreated on the stage." Serena broke in, "With a white arbor just covered with roses. The chairs will be white, like the metal ones you see on patios. The Caronsburg Star Theater has quite a nice stage, and we have a lot of friends from the Drama group who are going to do it up royally."

And don't forget, Mrs. Lilac," Rose broke in, "you are allowed to bring a guest. It would be nice if you had a well dressed gentleman to escort you. And if you don't have someone, we will certainly be able to find one of Bernie's young friends who will be happy to escort an older woman."

Mrs. Lilac smiled. She was glad for the brief bit of humor, for she was on edge for the rest of the reading, just thinking about stepping out on that stage to read her poem. And of all times, both Serena and Rose had a hundred questions to ask her. She laid out spread after spread until she thought she was a robot. She had no idea how she ever managed to get through the final layouts, but she did. When mother and daughter were gone, Mrs. Lilac nearly fell apart. She sat at the table and held her head in her hands. She was nearly exhausted and close to tears. Oh, it wasn't just the thought of reading her poem in front of a lot of people, it was the past weeks and everything both good and bad that had happened to her. She was usually not prone to anxiety attacks, but if ever she was close to one, it was now. She had to find a way to calm down a bit.

By this time it was dark, and she took Scrappy and went out into the fragrant May night. The stars overhead were brilliant, and for a moment she stood in the center of the yard and looked up at them and thought of the galaxies and galaxies that lay beyond her sight. Surely in this one small world she inhabited, she could find a circle of peace.

They walked down to Rainbow River, and Mrs. Lilac sank into a chair she had pulled up to the edge of the stream. Scrappy sensed her fatigue, for he demanded very little and was content to lie next to her as she sat there in the dark and smelled the fragrant air and listened to the singing of the water.

She had no idea how long she sat there, but she finally came back to herself, pulled herself up from the chair and made her way back to the cottage. They were just going in the front door when she heard a vehicle pull into the driveway. She turned and saw that it was Mr. Gately. She grew quite tense again wondering what news he had to tell her of his wife.

He came up to her, and she saw at once there was a look of relief on his face. Before they could go inside, he reached out and took Mrs. Lilac's hand.

"I've wanted to come talk to you before this," he said, "but so much has happened. And tonight I felt I just had to come and thank you. You saved my wife's life."

"Oh, no, I didn't," she protested, as they went inside and she closed the door. "I just gave you some advice. I just told you what I could see in the cards."

"I did exactly as you told me," he said, excitedly. "I went to the hospital that night, and I'm afraid I was quite a holy terror. I had them all hopping. I told her doctor if he stopped the transfusions I would sue them all, including the hospital. They did what I told them to, and by morning she had stabilized, and the bleeding had stopped. She's coming home at the end of the week."

"That's wonderful news," Mrs. Lilac exclaimed. "I'm so happy for you! It's a terrible tragedy to lose someone you love, and I'm so glad you haven't lost her."

"I'm as happy as I can ever remember," Mrs. Lilac," Mr. Gately told her. "And it's all because you took the time to read your cards for me."

"It's what I do, Mr. Gately. It's what I've done. I try to make a difference in people's lives. Is that so terrible? Is that the evil I'm accused of?"

"It was wrong of me to listen to what people were saying about you," Mr. Gately said, his eyes lowered. "I guess it was easier than taking the time to get to know you. But I'm a busy person. I have a lot on my mind every day. I was more concerned over my business than I was over thinking of you as a human being. I'm sorry for that. But then, I guess like everyone else, when you are at the end of your rope, you turn in unexpected directions for help."

"Would you like some coffee?" Mrs. Lilac asked, suddenly feeling that she needed something to get her through until bedtime. It had been quite a day.

When the coffee was ready, and she had served them both a large mug full, Mr. Gately rubbed his hands together and looked at her.

"The truth is, Mrs. Lilac, I don't want you to leave the cottage. It's your home and I'll make sure you don't have this worry over you anymore. I guess I didn't realize how hard it would be for you, and what a situation I was putting you in. But I want to make up for it now. Perhaps you feel you didn't do much to help me or my wife, but I know you did, and that's all that matters."

Mrs. Lilac could hardly believe what she was hearing. It seemed a dream for a moment, and she sat there staring at Mr. Gately, staring at his hands, his face, his eyes, to be sure he was a real person and not just a phantom she had conjured up in her mind. Then she began to cry, the tears running down her cheeks like a stream. Relieved and embarrassed at the same time, she grabbed a tissue from the box on the table and dabbed at her face. Scrappy jumped into her lap and tried licking away the tears. She couldn't think of a word to say, and she sat there sobbing quietly while Mr. Gately went on with what he was telling her.

"I'll come up with a way to lease the cottage to you for life, if necessary. I could even deed this piece of property and sell it to you for a reasonable price. I'll find a way, but whatever I do, there won't be anything more for you to worry about. The cottage is yours, from here on in. You've already made it a home."

Mr. Gately left her then. She managed to thank him as he was leaving, but she sat there in the chair for a long time trying to let the truth of his words sink in. She had never been a person with any high expectations of life, living it as simply as possible was what she had always tried to do for herself. But she couldn't think of another thing that had made her as happy as what Mr. Gately had just told her. She looked about the living room. There was Fern's huge daisy painting above the sofa, there was her mother's oak buffet, there was the old yellow cabinet that held her tea cup collection, and there was

Scrappy and Stormy lying together asleep on the sofa. Their lives had never missed a beat, but now they could live out the rest of their years in this place that was as much their home as it was hers. It was strange to feel as though her sight, both physical and mental, had suddenly cleared, and she could actually see again after too long a time.

Mrs. Lilac slept very little that night. She tried very hard, and once or twice she fell into a dream state, but every time she did, she came back to herself and heard or saw the familiar borders of wakefulness. Not long after daylight, she sighed and got out of bed. Sleep would no doubt come at some point. She would probably drop from exhaustion before the end of the day, but there was no sense trying to force anything.

Just after nine o'clock she rang Fern's number. She could hear it ring and ring until finally Fern's sleepy voice said, "Hello."

"I'm so sorry to wake you Fern, but I had to call. Mr. Gately came last night and gave me the news that I don't have to leave. It's a long story, but I'll fill you in when I see you again."

"I'm so happy for you," Fern said, her voice suddenly awake. "It would have been good for me to have you live right down the street, but I know where your heart is, and there it will stay. I'll let Mrs Kendall know. I'm sure she'll be alright with it, and she will be happy for you, also."

Mrs. Lilac also called Wanda and Julie. Wanda answered the phone. There was a scream on the other end of the line when Mrs. Lilac told her the news.

"Boy, we'll have something to celebrate now," she said, excitedly. "Julie and I will have to come up with something special to go with this surprise!"

After that, Mrs. Lilac called some of her more regular clients to let them know what had happened. Everyone was pleased that they would continue seeing her in the same familiar setting. Finally, she rang Bill Green's number. He answered at once and seemed very happy to hear from her.

"I'm so glad for you," he said, when Mrs. Lilac had told him her story. "I had a feeling something would change for you. I just couldn't see you living anywhere else."

Later that afternoon he came to see her. She hadn't started her readings as it was just after three, so they took Scrappy down to the stream for a walk. It was a rare and beautiful May day.

Off across the meadow the pale green trees had grown more full at a surprising rate, and were interspersed with blossoming trees and bushes in shades of pink and white.

"You have a beautiful view here," he told her, as they stood there watching the sunlight sparkle on the swift stream.

Yes it is quite a lovely view." she told him, "especially at this time of year."

"You love water, I can tell," Bill Green said. "Well there's a place I'd like to take you one of these days soon. It's called Mountain Valley Lake. Would you like to see it?"

"I would love to," she said. "Just let me know when. And by the way, I have something to ask you also. I have a wedding to go to next month. It's on the 26th. It's one of my clients, and I have to read a poem I've written for it. But you see, I need an escort. I wonder if you would consider..."

"Of course I'll go with you," he said. " I would be honored."

After that, there was nothing to say. Mrs. Lilac stood very still taking it all in, the meadow in all its seasonal finery, the pets sitting very still together looking across the stream, and Bill Green standing so close she could hear his breathing, regular and sure. She wondered if he was as aware of her. She certainly hoped he couldn't hear her heartbeat, for it seemed wild and nearly out of control.

JUNE

And June is never really over, for buried deep in every living thing, in the trees and the grass, the birds and the insects, buried in our hearts is a pattern and a longing to return to this place of warmth and deep contentment, this place that holds the promise and fulfillment of our life and purpose in being. And with the memory of June in our hearts, we can travel on knowing the surety of life continuing and of our own ultimate return.

From Mrs. Lilac's Journal

On a bright June morning, Mrs. Lilac stood on the creek bank and watched the mallards drift by on the current. A few moments earlier a mother and eight babies passed before her, the ducklings staying as close the mother as they could. She was surprised that Scrappy sat very still watching them, his head moving from side to side as though he wasn't quite sure what he was seeing. Off across the meadow, the greening year had nearly reached a peak of unfurling leaves, and the cows drifted closer each day. She was sure that in only a short time they would be standing at the fence opposite, staring at her.

Mrs. Lilac breathed deeply of the warming air. It smelled of summer and time, so hard to describe the essences of the countryside. Birds were everywhere. She particularly enjoyed the robins who were here in numbers larger than she could remember. Often the birds swooped low over the stream, then rose quickly into the air with a sudden flash of wing.

It was the first time in months that Mrs. Lilac could just stand, sit, or be, enjoying the land she had grown to love. The worries and fears of the last months had been lifted from her by Mr. Gately's visit. Since then she had, day by day, been trying to grow into her new found freedom.

The summer was yet to come and lay before her, ripe and promising. Only the wedding, in a few weeks, was a major challenge for her.

The day before, a colorful invitation had come in the mail from Wanda and Julie. They were having a Fiesta Party in their back yard, "in honor of Mrs. Lilac." It was to be on Saturday evening, the following week, and luckily she had nothing else on her calendar. The girls were impulsive, and certainly hadn't given her a lot of time to think about it.

Wanda did call later that afternoon to ask if she was able to come.

"I know I didn't give you a lot of time to decide." Wanda said, excitedly. "But we wanted to have something to celebrate your good news and decided to have it in your honor."

"Well, that's certainly kind of you," Mrs. Lilac told her. "But I have just one request. I do not want to read any cards that evening. For once, I just want to be myself and try to have a good time."

"Of, course dear, we didn't expect that anyway." Wanda said. "We're just going to eat and have fun."

Her first client that afternoon was Twila Marchand. She greeted Mrs. Lilac on the porch with a hug. "It's good to see you," she said, excitedly.

"And you too," Mrs. Lilac told her, noticing the sparkle in the young ladies eye. She was dressed smartly in black slacks and a blue blouse and was sporting a new hairdo, a short, wavy look.

"There's someone I want you to meet, Mrs. Lilac," she said, taking her by the hand to lead her down the drive to where her car was parked. For the first time, Mrs. Lilac noticed the young man sitting in the passenger seat. He stepped out as the two of them came up to him. He was tall and blond and had a friendly face. He had on jeans and a green pullover shirt.

This is Joel Blackwell," Twila told her. "Joel, this is my friend, Mrs. Lilac."

"It's good to finally meet you," Joel said, shaking her hand in a very strong grip. "Twila's told me a lot about you."

"So nice to meet you, too," Mrs. Lilac said, thinking to herself that he seemed quite a good person. She was excellent with first impressions, and could instantly see that the young man already had strong feelings for her friend.

Joel waited in the car while Twila and Mrs. Lilac went inside.

What do you think, Mrs Lilac?" Twila blurted excitedly, when they were seated at the table. "I met him a couple of months ago, a blind date. We've had a great time getting to know each other. He's in banking, a real financial whiz!"

"My first impression is a good one. I feel there's a chemistry between the two of you."

"I think so, too, Mrs. Lilac." Twila said. "I think he's the one. I already see us down the road somewhere making serious decisions about things. Do you remember what you predicted the last time you read for me?"

"Yes, I do," Mrs. Lilac told her. "I saw a ring and a wedding. And I also saw a little girl and boy."

"When do you think it will be Mrs. Lilac?"

Mrs. Lilac consulted the cards. She was quite excited, and when she lay them out she understood why.

"I think it will be next year," Mrs. Lilac told her. "You know I have a wedding this month, and next year there will be another. Maybe it's a tradition that year after year I'll be invited to the weddings of my clients. Please don't ask me to recite a poem, though, the thought of doing that this time has me a nervous wreck."

"I'm sure you'll do well," Twila said. "You have a natural talent for being in the spotlight. You just don't realize it."

"Seriously," Mrs. Lilac said, going on with the reading, "I do see this as a very special relationship. I feel very strongly that this is the one for you. I see the ring by Fall. I'm so glad that you have put that other tragic relationship behind you. Oftentimes, the universe gives us something new if we just have the courage to move on from the old."

"Yes, I agree," Twila said, her voice serious. "It was hard for me to give up a relationship that I had such high hopes for, for such a long time. And maybe I didn't give myself enough time to heal, but Joel has done me a world of good. And I told him the complete story. He's been good about it, and seems to understand what I've been through."

"I had some good news," Mrs. Lilac, said, when the reading for Twila was finished. "My landlord has changed his mind. I don't have to move."

"I'm so glad," Twila exclaimed, "I thought it was possible that things would change, and I know that must be a real relief for you."

"You can't imagine the joy I feel," Mrs. Lilac told her.

"And what about the relationship thing you hinted at when I was here last?" Twila asked. "If I didn't know better, I'd think by the twinkle in your eyes today that it's on again."

"There might be a change in that direction," Mrs. Lilac laughed.

"If we're not careful, I may be a wedding guest myself before too long," Twila remarked.

"Let's not go that far," Mrs. Lilac said, taking the time to lower her eyes and gather up the cards.

"We'll let time take care of that," Twila said, as she got up from the table.

"And though I'm sure I'll see you before then, we have a date for a wedding next year."

Mrs. Lilac hugged Twila fondly and kissed her cheek. After she left, Mrs. Lilac sat still for a moment watching the sunlight as it ebbed at the window. Strange the way life happened with its light and shadows. She was glad for Twila and extremely happy the future seemed to hold such promise for her. She was happy, too, for herself, though she had no great expectations of anything. It was enough that one day would follow another and she would willingly accept whatever joy or sorrow came her way. Life was made of small things, and as she grew older, bits of promise were better than faded dreams and disillusionments.

Mrs Lilac had thought of asking Bill Green to go with her to Wanda and Julie's party, but since she had already invited him to escort her to the wedding, and he had asked her to go with him to lake, she thought it best not to overdo things. So on a pleasant June evening she drove alone toward town. Fern had called, and she was to pick up her friend around seven. The girls didn't actually live in Caronsburg, but in a small village called Farmington, a few miles to the east. They lived in a quaint log house that had seen several additions over the years and seemed to drift off in many directions, but was quite a homey place, with beautiful landscaping and a back yard that ran some distance before ending at a grove of trees.

Mrs. Lilac had worn plain blue slacks and a white blouse and had brought a sweater as the party would be outdoors. Fern, too, had dressed rather conservatively, and she told Mrs. Lilac that she was sure Wanda and Julie would do enough dressing for all of them.

When they arrived at the party, however, they were greeted by Wanda who was attired normally in shorts and a blouse, with the exception of a fake grass skirt worn around her waist. Mrs. Lilac had never seen Wanda's hair look so attractive.. She must have had it permed recently, and it lay in small curls all around her head.

"Julie's in the yard," Wanda said, as she escorted them through the house to the patio.

There were several guests there already, and the yard was quite a sight. Patio lights and paper lanterns hung from the trees. There were also lit torches at various spots, and Hawaiian music played from somewhere. The food tables and beverage bar were set up on the patio itself, and lawn chairs and chaises were grouped in comfortable spots around the yard.

"Come meet Mother and the dogs, " Wanda said, and led them to the corner of the patio, where a tall dignified lady in white hair sat on a lawn chair, with a Boston Terrier in her lap. Lying at her feet were two others.

"This is my mother, Florence," Wanda said. "And this is Bo, Dixie, and Otie."

"So good to meet you," Mrs. Lilac told her, extending her hand.

"I"m happy to meet you also," Florence said. "The girls talk about you all the time. I've asked them often to invite you out, but sometimes they are so far out there, I don't know if they are coming or going."

It was obvious to Mrs. Lilac that Florence was a little more conservative and sedate than the two girls. She seemed serene in her world, almost like an empress, and the dogs, so silent and well behaved, obviously adored her.

"Where's Julie?" Fern suddenly asked.

"Wanda burst into laughter. "Come on," she said, "I'll take you to her."

She led them to the back of the yard where a Gazebo sat at the center. It was surrounded by multicolored garden lights and a huge sign was placed at the front. MRS. CRABAPPLE,

PSYCHIC ADVISOR it said. READINGS 1.00. At the center of the Gazebo, behind a small round table with a purple cloth and a crystal ball, sat Julie. She wore a fancy red bandanna around her head, and was dressed in a red lace dress with frilly long sleeves. She had on huge gold hoop earrings, and had red fingernails that looked at least two inches long. She had a serious look on her face, but was struggling hard not to laugh.

"Since you didn't want to read cards tonight," Mrs. Lilac," Wanda said, "we brought in a guest reader. What do you think?"

Mrs. Lilac couldn't speak, and immediately burst into laughter. Even Fern found the whole thing amusing.

"Since you are the guest of honor, Mrs. Lilac," Wanda told her, "I think you should be the first to have your fortune read."

Do you think I could wait until later?" Mrs. Lilac asked. "I'm a bit hungry just now, and a drink might be nice. I think I'd better fortify myself a bit to get ready for this."

"That will be fine," Wanda said, "but this is something you have to do before leaving."

As she led them away, the guest reader had her hand over her mouth trying to hide an audible chuckle.

It turned out to be quite a pleasant party. There were a lot of guests. The yard seemed full of people, and voices rose from different directions, wafted on the pleasantly scented air. Mrs. Lilac and Fern found comfortable chairs in a corner where they enjoyed the food and a wonderful tropical punch, non alcoholic, as the hostess informed them. It had been made from various fruit juices and had a delicious lemony zing. The food was quite an array of everything from a delicious seafood salad, to hamburgers on the grill. Wanda made quite an impressive cook, standing by the barbecue grill, cooking to order.

Several people she hadn't met came up and introduced themselves to Mrs. Lilac. Even "Mrs. Crabapple", between her "readings", came and mingled with the guests. The music went on continuously, both orchestral and vocals. Mrs. Lilac couldn't remember when she'd had such a pleasant time, all the fears and worries of the past months were gone, hopefully for good.

At some point "Mrs." Crabapple" came up and whispered in her ear. "It's time for your reading now."

So with a deep sigh of acceptance, Mrs. Lilac was led back through the crowded yard to the Gazebo, where she allowed herself to be seated in a comfortable wicker chair at the front of the table. The guest reader could hardly contain herself. She took a large deck of Tarot cards into her hands and began laying them out in some sort of spread even Mrs. Lilac had never used. "Mrs. Crabapple's voice came out as part laugh, part screech. All in all it was quite a revelation.

"I see great happiness ahead for you," "Mrs. Crabapple" began. "You have had much sorrow and heartbreak, but the Goddess of the universe has decided it is time for you to be happy. She has many wonderful things in store for you. There is money, power, fame and oh, my goodness, none the least of which is love." She paused a moment and stared into the crystal ball. "I see a tall man before you who is staring at you lovingly. He reaches out his hand and takes yours in his. He asks you to marry him."

"Mrs. Crabapple" paused a moment and stared at the cards. "And you look at him for a long moment and finally say, Yes!"

Mrs. Lilac didn't know whether to laugh or run. Julie made quite a picture as the Gypsy reader. She was quite the actress, so much so that Mrs. Lilac felt chills run up her arms. She understood from just this little play acting Julie was doing, how easily it was to be pulled into having your fortune told. The reader had more power than she deserved, especially when she might be trying to hoodwink her client. She realized Julie was only trying to lighten her spirits, that she couldn't know the secret of how Bill Green had come into her life and how much her feelings for him had grown over the last months. She did know marriage was not a part of what she could see of their future. Just being close friends was enough for her to hope for.

When the reading was finished, Mrs. Lilac hugged Julie and told her what a fine job she'd done. Julie was laughing and couldn't contain herself.

Later, when it was time to go home, Wanda and Julie called all the guests together, and Wanda gave a small speech.

"The party tonight was in honor of our dear friend, Mrs. Lilac," she told them. "She has brought so much hope and joy to so many people. Julie and I owe her so much. She has recently received the best news she could hope for, that she doesn't have to move from her home, and that is the main reason we are celebrating here tonight. We hope she will continue to be happy there as long as she lives."

With that, she handed Mrs. Lilac a painted plaque.. There was a white angel at the center and above her the word BELIEVE.

"This is for you," Wanda and Julie said together. "It's for your home. Your home that will always be your home."

"There was a pause in which Mrs. Lilac swallowed tears and tried to find the right words to say. "Thank you with all my heart," she said finally, hugging the girls.

"We love you Mrs. Lilac." Wanda and Julie said, and there was applause from all around.

June seemed to speed up, and before she knew it, the wedding was only two weeks away. Mrs. Lilac found some time to go shopping and picked up the shoes and hat needed for her outfit.

The hat was quite a sight, and when she got it home, she stood before her vanity mirror and modeled it again. It was purple and had a wide brim, and the whole thing was covered with frilly lace to match. She wasn't sure she totally approved, but it was the best she could come up with and would have to do.

She finally made plans with Bill Green for their drive to the lake. It happened on a Sunday, and Mrs. Lilac was quite nervous as she dressed in a simple pair of tan slacks and a flowered blouse. She put on a pair of comfortable shoes, as there would probably be some walking involved. Outside, the weather was again perfect. The sun shone brightly from a flawless sky, and she was happy to see there wasn't a cloud in sight.

She took Scrappy into the yard for a walk while they waited for Bill Green. He seemed to know she was going somewhere and had his back up a bit, but he, too, was fascinated with the weather and soon forgot his anxiety over her leaving. June had been mostly lovely so far, but a few days before, a huge thunder storm had blown up during the night and had given her a good scare. The wind had been fierce, and the rain had poured so loudly on the roof, that Mrs. Lilac asked the universe for protection. But then, the next morning, the sun came out again, and the world took on the incredible air of June. The scent of honeysuckle and wild roses came to her across the fence, reminding her it was one of the loveliest fragrances the year had to offer.

Bill Green pulled into her driveway in a car she didn't recognize. It was dark blue and shone with a luster that caught the sunlight and seemed to sparkle like diamonds. It had a thin white strip around the front, and the whole thing looked in mint condition.

"What a beautiful car." Mrs. Lilac said as he got out and came around to open the door for her. He was dressed in jeans and a blue pullover shirt.

"It's a 1968 Camaro Rally Sport. " Bill Green told her. "I restored it myself. I only drive it on special occasions. I thought today would be a good day to take her out for a spin."

Mrs. Lilac saw a look in his eyes that was only put there by admiration for something special, something that might have been a dream that with patience became reality. For the first time, she saw a many faceted man who was beginning to step outside a wall of grief that had held him prisoner for too long.

The drive to the lake was quite an exciting one. The farms and valleys rolled away on either side of them, as incredible vistas opened up at every angle. Blossoming trees and bushes were everywhere. Farms and streams and newly planted fields left Mrs. Lilac in awe. There was small talk between she and Bill Green, but he seemed to realize how caught up she was by the fantastic views, and was silent while she enjoyed the scenes that lay around every turn.

There was a short drive up a steep winding road, and then suddenly she could see flashes of blue through the trees. They had reached the lake, and Mrs. Lilac was stunned by the size of it. Bill Green parked his Camaro Rally Sport in a parking area and helped her out of the car. He took her arm as they went down the path through groves of pine trees to the water.

The lake lay before them, ringed round by deep forests of pine and other trees. A steep ridge rose beyond the far shore. Several small boats dotted the water, and she could see a few fisherman at various places along the near shoreline.

"Let's walk along the path for awhile," Bill Green said. "Let me know if you get tired."

He held onto her arm as they walked. Mrs. Lilac couldn't remember when she'd seen a body of water that was so astoundingly beautiful. The air was the purest she had breathed for awhile, and she took great gulps of it. The scent was that of woods and water and the mysterious processes of time. They walked for quite a distance and suddenly came across a promontory of land that reached out into the lake. It was surrounded by a stone wall and was used for fishing and picnicking. There were several picnic tables at the far end.

Bill Green led her up to one of them and they sat together facing the lake.

"Thank you for bringing me here," Mrs. Lilac told him. "I don't remember when I last saw anything quite so incredible. I don't go many places by myself anymore, and it's a shame that we miss so much through business and overwork."

"Yes it is," Bill Green said. "Time is certainly the enemy." He paused for a moment and then looked at her, his eyes glancing down. It was as though he wanted to tell her something but was afraid to.

"Betty," he said finally, "I want to say something to you, and it may come out all wrong. But I have to say it anyway. I'm not over my wife. I don't know if I ever will be over her. It's hard to erase thirty years. But I like you. I feel something for you that even I don't understand. And it's not just because you tried to help me and understood what I was going through. The truth is, I want to see you Betty. At our age, dating doesn't seem to be quite an appropriate word. And I mean I won't want to see other people, just you, as long and as often as you allow."

Mrs. Lilac was suddenly just a mass of jelly. It was impossible to control the flood of emotions that washed over her. Tears began to stream down her face, and she grabbed her purse and found a tissue, and held it momentarily to her soggy eyes.

I didn't mean to make you cry," he said, reaching across to take her hand.

"They are happy tears," she told him.

"Do you have anything to say?" he asked, looking into her eyes.

"I would like seeing you very much," Mrs. Lilac said, her voice weak. "I can't think of anything I'd like better."

The day of Serena and Bernie's wedding finally dawned. By this time, Mrs. Lilac was a nervous wreck. She went through the usual daily agenda as absentminded as she could ever remember. She kept losing things, and checked and rechecked her purse to see if she had everything together. The one thing she always checked for was the crude stone heart Annabelle had given her that day. Each time she saw it, she could hear Annabelle's voice saying, "Luck and love, honey, that's what I'm wishin' for you." She would always carry it with her.

She tried keeping her focus on Scrappy, who wanted in and out a dozen times before it was time for her to get dressed for the event. And each time they went out, she would concentrate on the yard, the creek bank, and the meadow. Being at home felt so good to her there were times she could barely speak. And now there was Bill Green to think of. She had been giddy as a school girl since their trip to the lake, and already they had planned several special things to do together in the coming weeks. He was now calling her every day, and there was something so special and comforting to hear his voice the first thing in the morning or the last thing at night.

Mrs. Lilac was dressed and ready when he arrived around one. From what she could see in the mirror, the outfit looked a bit gaudy, but wearing a costume was nothing new to her. The ceremony was scheduled for two o'clock, but she needed to be there early to find her spot and become oriented to how things would proceed. There had not been a full rehearsal of the speakers the day before, because the theater had not been available, and this only increased her nervousness. She was so afraid her voice would fail her at the last moment.

Bill Green was once again driving the blue Camaro Rally Sport. He was dressed in a dark blue suit with a red tie, and looked quite handsome. She told him so.

"And you look lovely, Betty," he said, as Mrs. Lilac stood there. Before opening the door for her, he leaned down and gently kissed her cheek. Mrs. Lilac took his hand and squeezed it.

Bill Green drove them into town and found a parking spot in a lot across the street from the Caronsburg Star Theater. The marquee was lit, and it said in large letters, Best Wishes, Serena and Bernie. The lobby of the theater was filled with flowers. A harpist was playing at the back of the lobby area, and all the way down the aisle, Mrs. Lilac heard the faint tinkling of the strings.

Rose Wilder was waiting for them at the side entrance to the backstage area. She seemed disoriented and out of breath.

"Oh Mrs. Lilac," she cried. "I think I'm going to fall apart." She stopped a moment and touched Mrs. Lilac's arm. "You are a vision to behold." She went on without a beat. "You look lovely! That outfit is stunning!"

She pinned a purple corsage of orchids to the buttonhole of Mrs. Lilac's jacket. " There, that really sets the whole thing off," she said. Rose suddenly noticed Bill Green, and as nervous and out of breath as she was, she stepped back for a moment and stared at him, and then glanced at Mrs. Lilac.

"And who is this?" she asked, in her calmest voice.

"This is my friend, Bill Green," Mrs. Lilac told her. "And Bill this is Rose Wilder, the mother of the bride."

They were both cordial to each other, and Mrs. Lilac knew Rose was interested in knowing more about her handsome escort, but she suddenly went back into her nervous mode and took Mrs. Lilac's arm. "I've got to get you backstage," she told her.

"And Mr. Green," Rose told him, "you can sit anywhere on this side where there are no reserved signs."

"I'll see you afterward, Betty," Bill said, squeezing her hand as he left her.

The backstage area was alive with activity. Mrs. Lilac was almost dizzy from the smell of flowers. The scent wafted everywhere. Rose led her onto the stage, and Mrs. Lilac was speechless. She had never seen so many roses. They climbed everywhere. There were several trellises and an arbor, and a huge fountain in the center of the stage.

"When you read your poem, you will stand just here." Rose said, leading to a lectern that sat on the right side of the stage. There was a twin one on the opposite side, and Rose explained there would be readings from both areas. A Master of Ceremonies would introduce her when it was her time to recite. "And then when you're finished with your poem, you just sit here," she went on, indicating one of two garden chairs in front of a rose covered trellis.

Finally, Rose led her to a dressing area where there were several chairs, and Mrs. Lilac sank into one and caught her breath. It was very hot, and she hoped the air conditioning system would soon kick in. Her nerves reached a peak of sensitivity. For a moment she thought she would collapse, but then, she began to notice other people arriving for the ceremony. Three or four of them sat with her in the waiting area. She assumed they would also have songs or recitals to perform. She suddenly felt a kind of peace settle over her. Whatever would be, would be, and there was life beyond this wedding. She tried concentrating on what was happening.

By her watch, at exactly two o'clock, the organ started to play, and she heard a beautiful soprano voice begin to sing a love song she had never heard before. It spoke of trust and happiness, of youthful love, and all the promises we make to each other. It was beautifully done.

Then there was a long recital of the theater organ, stunningly performed by a gentleman who had played it during films and special events for over twenty five years. The songs were mostly familiar ones, True Love, Promise me, Love is a many splendored thing, on and on. The music rang throughout the theater and Mrs. Lilac loved every moment of the recital. It certainly helped put her in a better frame of mind.

Finally, she heard the strains of the wedding march, and she could only imagine the wedding party slowly making its way down the aisle. Then, at last, there were the sounds of the bridal procession, and she could hear the gasps from the audience as the bride made her way to the stage.

Then there was silence, and the sound of the MC as he began to introduce the speakers. One gentleman read a piece from the bible, another read excerpts from the favorite authors of the bride and groom. The soloist sang another beautiful song, all about love flowing steadily across the years. And then she heard a voice saying, "And now, here is Mrs. Betty Lilac to read a poem, especially written for the bride and groom."

She stood up, as though she were a robot, and walked to the spot where the curtain was pulled aside, and stepped onto the stage. There was a hush as she walked to the lectern. For a moment, she looked to where Bernie and Serena were sitting before the fountain and arbor at the center of the stage. Serena was quite beautiful in a gown of white satin and lace. Bernie sat beside her in his blue tuxedo. She smiled at them and nodded her head. Then she turned and looked out into the audience. The theater was nearly filled. Her nervousness was gone. This was the present moment and she was still alive.

And then, with the voice of the finest dramatic actress, she began to speak.

"My Wish," she began, "For Serena and Bernie on their Wedding day."

After the good times and all of the bad times,
after the hard rock and the flowing stream,
after the fire on the mountain,
love is still there if we dream.

For a brief moment, Mrs. Lilac paused and looked out over the sea of faces before her. But she saw only one face, and it seemed to be surrounded by a halo of light. It was Bill Green's face, and she could see that he was smiling.

CPSIA information can be obtained at www.ICGtesting.com
Printed in the USA
BVOW05s1354110914

366328BV00001B/37/P